A DADDY
FOR HER SONS

Warwickshire County Council

NEW SEP 13	LIL		
21 JUN 16 *			
13 FEB 2020			

This item is to be returned or renewed before the latest date above. It may be borrowed for a further period if not in demand. **To renew your books:**

- **Phone the 24/7 Renewal Line 01926 499273 or**
- **Visit www.warwickshire.gov.uk/libraries**

Discover • Imagine • Learn • *with libraries*

Warwickshire County Council

A DADDY
FOR HER SONS

BY

RAYE MORGAN

MILLS
BOON®

First published in Great Britain 2013
by Mills & Boon, an imprint of Harlequin (UK) Limited.
Large Print edition 2013
Harlequin (UK) Limited, Eton House,
18-24 Paradise Road, Richmond, Surrey TW9 1SR

© Helen Conrad 2013

ISBN: 978 0 263 23681 1

Harlequin (UK) policy is to use papers that are natural,
renewable and recyclable products and made from
wood grown in sustainable forests. The logging and
manufacturing process conform to the legal environmental
regulations of the country of origin.

Printed and bound in Great Britain
by CPI Antony Rowe, Chippenham, Wiltshire

This is dedicated to Lauri, for everything wonderful that comes out of her oven!

CHAPTER ONE

A NIGHTMARE. That was what this had to be. She must be dreaming. But what had she expected from a blind date?

Jill Darling was no shy innocent, but her face was blazing. She could feel it. The man was trying to… Ugh, it was just too creepy to even try to name what he was doing. She couldn't really be sure unless she took a look under the table. And that would cause a scene. She couldn't do that. She knew people in this restaurant.

But…was that really his foot sliding up and down her leg?

He was leaning close, talking on and on, his breath hot on her neck. Okay, maybe that was all in the game. But what the heck was that foot doing?

She tried to move away, but she was trapped,

huddled right up against the edge of the planter that sat right beside their table, tickling her nose with its palm fronds. They were eating in the restaurant of the nicest hotel in this part of town. It had Irish linen tablecloths, real sterling silverware and a small combo playing for dancers on a tiny dance floor to the side.

She took a long drink from her water glass, then looked over at him. She tried to smile, but she knew it was wobbly and pretty darn unconvincing if he should happen to actually notice it.

Karl Attkins was his name. Her friend's brother. He was good looking enough, but somehow cold, as though she could have been anyone with an "available female" label stamped on her forehead. Should she ask him about the foot? And maybe warn him not to lose sight of his shoe. It wouldn't be easy to replace that here in this crowded restaurant.

Oh, Lord, he was using his toes now. She was going to have to say something. If she didn't, her nice steak dinner just might come back up.

And all that wine she drank, trying to keep busy. This just wasn't cool. She took a deep breath and tried to think of a way to say it without being insulting.

But then he gave her the out she needed.

"Would you like to dance?" he asked, cocking an eyebrow as though he knew she must consider him quite debonair.

Dance. No, not at all. But she steeled herself to the effort. Dancing ought to give him a reason to put his shoe back on, and if so, it would all be worth it.

"Sure," she said breathlessly. "Why not?"

Well, the fact that they were playing a tango at that very moment might have been a reason to sit this one out. But it hardly mattered. At least the man was shod once more. She tried to keep the electric smile painted on her face as he led her to the proper position. And then she glanced at her watch and wondered how much longer she was going to have to endure this torture. She had to put in a good chunk of time or the friends who'd got her into this wouldn't believe she'd really tried.

Oh, Mary Ellen, she groaned silently as Karl pushed her to and fro dramatically across the dancing floor, leaving her to lunge about like a puppet with its strings cut. *I love you dearly, but this is just too high a price to pay for your friendship.*

"But, Jill," all her friends had counseled solemnly, "you've got to do it. You've got to get back into the swim of things. It's been over a year since Brad...well, since you've been alone." The timing had helped make her receptive. Changes were making her feel vulnerable. Her sister was probably moving away, and her younger half-sister had recently died. Loneliness was looming large in her life. "Time is streaking by," another friend lectured. "Don't let it leave you behind. Don't be a coward. Get out there and fight!"

Fight? For what?

"A man, of course," said Mary Ellen. "Once

you hit your age, they don't come a dime a dozen any more. You've got competition."

"But, what if I...?"

"No! You can't give up!" her friend Crystal had chimed in. "Your kids need a father figure in the home."

Mary Ellen had fixed her with a steely stare. "And you want to show old Brad, don't you?"

Show old Brad. The need to do just that surged in her. Of course she wanted to show old Brad. Sure. She would date. If he could do it, so could she. Stand back. She was ready for the challenge.

But where would she find someone to date? Mary Ellen knew just the man for her.

"My brother Karl is a real player," she said airily. "He'll get you back into the swing of things in no time. He has so many friends. You'll be dating like crazy before you know it."

Dating. She remembered dating. The way your heart raced as you waited for him to come to the door, the shy pauses, the way your eyes met his and then looked quickly away. Would he kiss you on the doorstep? Were you really going to let him?

Fun!

But that was then. This was a completely different thing, seemingly from a galaxy far, far away. She was older now. She'd been married and she had two kids. She knew how things worked. She could handle it. Or so she thought.

No. This was a nightmare.

At least her dress was pretty, and she didn't get many chances to wear something like this anymore. A sleek shift dress in teal-blue, it was covered with sequins and glistened as she walked, making her feel sexy and pretty and nice. Too bad she was wasting that on a man who spent more time looking at himself in the mirror than she did.

The tango was over. She turned back toward the table in relief, but Karl grabbed her free hand and twirled her around to face him. The band was playing a cha cha. He grinned. "Hey mambo!" he cried out and began to sway. He seemed to consider himself quite the ballroom dancer, even if he couldn't tell one Latin dance from another.

Jill had a decision to make. Would she rather dance, or go back to playing footsie? She wasn't sure she knew how to cha cha. But she knew she didn't want to feel that foot on her leg again.

What the hell.

"Everybody loves to cha-cha-cha," she murmured as she let him twirl her again.

And then she looked up and saw Connor Mc-Nair staring at her in horror.

Her blood ran cold. She was still moving, but no one could accuse her of dancing at this point. The music didn't mean a thing.

Connor. Oh, no.

First, it appalled her to think that anyone she knew might see her here like this. But close on that thought came the shock question—was Brad with him?

No. She glanced around quickly and didn't see

any sign of her ex-husband at all. Thank heaven for small blessings. Connor must have come to town and was staying here at the hotel—alone. But still, it was Connor, Brad's best friend, the one person most likely to report to him. She could hardly stand it.

He was mouthing something to her. She squinted, trying to make it out. What was he trying to say?

She couldn't tell, but he was coming out onto the dance floor. Why? She looked around, feeling wild, wanting to run. What was he going to do?

"May I cut in?" he asked Karl.

He was polite, but unsmiling, and Karl didn't seem to be in a friendly mood.

"What? No. Go get your own girl," Karl told him, frowning fiercely. And just to prove his point, he grabbed Jill and pulled her close.

She looked over his shoulder at Connor. He offered a safe harbor of sorts, but there was danger there, too. She didn't want to talk to Connor. She didn't want to have anyone close to Brad anywhere near. The pain of Brad's desertion still ached inside her like an open wound and she didn't want anyone from his side of the rift to see her like this—much less talk to her.

So she glared at Connor. Let him know she didn't need him or his rescue. She was doing fine. She was here enjoying herself. Sort of.

She got back to dancing, swaying her hips, making her sequins sparkle, and trying hard to smile at Karl. Let Connor see that she was having the time of her life. Let him take that bit of news back to Brad, if that was what he was after.

"Mambo!" she cried out, echoing Karl. Why the heck not?

Connor gave her a look of disbelief as he stepped back to the sidelines, but he didn't leave. The next dance was a simple two-step, but that meant Karl's arms around her again, and she couldn't disguise the shudder that gave her.

And there was Connor, taking in every nuance. She glowered at him. He was very handsome in his crisp white shirt with the dark slacks that looked tailor-made. But that was beside the point. Didn't he have a table to go to? What gave him the right to stand there and watch her? Biting her lip, she tried to keep him out of her line of vision and blot him out of her head.

But then he was back, right at Karl's elbow again, stopping them in their tracks.

"Excuse me," he said, looking very serious. "Listen, do you have a silver BMW in the parking lot?"

Karl blinked. His eyes narrowed suspiciously, but he couldn't resist the question. "Why, yes I do. What about it?"

Connor's brows came together in a look of sorrow. "I'm afraid your car's on fire."

Karl dropped Jill like a hot potato and whirled to face Connor. "What?" he cried, anguish contorting his face.

Connor was all sympathy. "I think they've

called the fire department, but you might want to get out there and…"

No more words were necessary. He was already gone.

Connor took Jill by the arm, looking annoyed when she balked and tried to pull away.

"Come on," he said impatiently. "I know a back way out."

Jill shook her head, not sure what he thought he was doing here. "But…I can't just leave."

Connor looked down at her and suddenly grinned, startling her. She'd forgotten how endearing he could be and she stared up at him. It was like finding a beloved forgotten toy in the attic. Affection for him trembled on the edge of her mood, but she batted it back.

"Why not?" he said. "Do you want to spend the next two hours with the guy?"

She tried to appear stern. She wanted to deny what he was implying. How could she go? What would she say to her friends? What would she tell Mary Ellen?

But in the end, his familiar grin did her in. "I'd rather eat dirt," she admitted, crumbling before him.

"There you go." He led her gently across the dance floor, only hesitating while she scooped up her sparkly little purse. They headed for the exit and he winked at a waiter who was holding the door for them, obviously primed to help with the escape. He paused only long enough to hand the man some folded money and then they were out the door.

"But what about his car?" Jill asked, worrying a bit. She knew the sense of guilt would linger long after the evening was gone. "He loves that car."

"Don't give it a second thought," he advised, steering her toward his own souped-up, twenty-year-old Camaro, a car she remembered from the past, and pulling open the passenger door.

"His car isn't really on fire, is it?" she asked as she plunked down into the leather seat.

"No." He sank into the driver's seat and grinned at her again. "Look, I'll do a lot for an old friend, but setting a guy's car on fire...no, that's a step too far."

She watched him start the engine and turn toward the back exit.

"But you will lie to him about it," she noted.

"Oh, yeah."

She sighed and settled back into the seat. All in all, at least she didn't have a naked foot exploring her leg at the moment. That alone was worth its weight in gold.

"Rickey's on the Bay?" he asked in the shorthand they both remembered from earlier years.

"Of course," she responded without thinking. That was where everyone always went when the night was still young enough to make the last ferry to the island. She turned and looked at the lights of Seattle in the distance. If only you could go back in time as easily as you could go back to the places where you hung out in your youth.

"I can't believe I'm letting you do this," she said with a sigh.

"I can't believe you needed me to do it."

She laughed. "Touché," she muttered. So much for the great date that was supposed to bring her out of her shell and into the social whirl.

She pulled her cell phone out of her purse and checked it.

"What are you doing?" Connor asked with just a hint of suspicion in his tone.

She glanced up at him and smiled impishly. "Waiting for Karl to call. I've got to explain this to him somehow."

He shuddered. "Is Karl the mambo king?" he asked.

She gave him a baleful look.

"Don't worry. I gave the waiter a little money to tell old Karl what the score was."

She raised an eyebrow. "And just what is the score, pray tell?"

He hesitated, then shrugged. "I told him to tell Karl I was a made guy from the mob and we didn't take kindly to outsiders poaching on our women."

"What?"

He looked a little embarrassed. "Yeah, I know. Definitely corny. But it was the best I could think of on the spur of the moment."

She had to hold back her laughter. He didn't deserve it.

"I didn't even know you were Italian."

"There are a lot of things you don't know about me." He gave her a mocking wink. "A lot of things you don't want to know."

"Obviously."

She frowned, thinking the situation over. "So now you've single-handedly destroyed my chances of dating anyone ever again in this town. Thanks a lot."

"I'm just looking out for you, sweetheart."

She rolled her eyes, but she was biting back a grin.

Rickey's was as flamboyant as a fifties retro diner should be, with bright turquoise upholstery and jukeboxes at every table. They walked in as though they ought to see a lot of old friends there, but no one looked the least bit familiar.

"We're old," he whispered in her ear as he led her to a booth along the side with windows on the marina. "Everyone we used to hang out with is gone."

"So why are we still here?" she asked, a bit grumpy about it. This was where so much of her life had played out in the old days. And now, the waitresses didn't know her and the faces all looked unfamiliar.

"Lost souls, searching for the meaning of life," he said, smiling at her across the linoleum-covered table. His smile looked wistful this time, unlike the cheerful grin from before.

"The meaning of life is clear enough," she protested. After all, hadn't everyone been lec-turing her on it for months? "Get on with things. Make the world a better place. Face reality and deal with it. Or something along those lines."

He shrugged. "Sounds nice, until you start

analyzing definitions. What exactly does 'better' mean? Better for whom? How do you get the whole world involved, anyway?"

She made a face at him. "You always were the great contrarian," she said accusingly. "And now I've let you kidnap me. Someone should call the police."

The waitress, a pretty young girl in a poodle skirt who'd just arrived at their table blanched and took a step backward.

"No, no," Jill told her quickly. "I'm only joking. Please don't take me seriously. Ever."

The waitress blinked rapidly, but risked a step closer in to take their order. She didn't hang around to chat, however.

"You scared her," Connor suggested as she hurried away.

"I scare everyone lately," Jill admitted. "What do you think? Am I too intense? Are my eyes a little wild?"

He looked at her uncertainly, not sure if the truth would be accepted in the spirit he would mean it. His gaze skimmed over her pretty face. She had new lines between the brows, a new hint of worry in her eyes. Her hands were clenched around her water glass, as though she were holding on to a life preserver. Tense was hardly a strong enough word. His heart broke just a little bit. What had happened to his care-free girl?

But that was just it. She wasn't "his," never had been.

He knew she'd been through a lot since Brad had left her. She had a right to a few ragged edges. But when you came right down to it, she was as beautiful as she'd ever been. Her golden hair sprang into curls in an untamed mass all around her head. Her dark eyes were still warm, her lips were still full and sexy. Still gorgeous after all these years.

And looking at her still sent him over the moon. It happened every time. She was like a substance he had to be careful he didn't mess with, knowing it would be too dangerous to overdose.

But he could see a difference in her and silently he swore at himself. Why had he stayed away so long? She probably could have used a friend. She'd lost her young girl sparkle and he regretted it. He loved that sparkle.

But now he frowned, studying her face as though he was worried about what he found there. "How are you doing, Jill?" he asked her quietly. "I mean really. How've you been?"

She sat back and really looked at him for the first time, a quiver of fear in her heart. This was what she really wanted to avoid. Silly banter was so much safer than going for truth.

She studied his handsome face, his crystal-blue eyes sparking diamond-like radiant light from between those inky black eyelashes that seemed too impossibly long. It had been over a year since she'd seen him last and he didn't seem quite so much like a kid living in a frat house anymore.

He'd always been such a contrast to Brad, like a younger brother who didn't want to grow up. Brad was the serious one, the ambitious one, the idea man who had the drive to follow through. Connor was more likely to be trying to make a flight to catch a party in Malibu or volunteering to crew on a sailing trip to Tahiti. Brad was a man you could count on. Connor—not so much.

Only that had turned out to be a lie, hadn't it? It was hard to trust anything much anymore once the man you'd considered your rock had melted away and wasn't there for you anymore.

She closed her eyes for a moment, then gave him a dazzling smile. "I've been great," she said breezily. "Life is good. The twins are healthy and my business is actually starting to make a profit, so we're good."

He didn't believe her. He'd known her too long to accept the changed woman she'd become. She'd always been careful—the responsible sort—but she'd also had a sense of fun, of carefree abandon. Instead, her eyes, her tone, her nervous movements, all displayed a wary tension, as though she was always looking over her shoulder to see what disaster might be gaining on her now.

"So good that you felt it was time to venture out into the dating world again, huh?" he noted, being careful to smile as he said it.

"Why not? I need to move on. I need to… to…" She couldn't remember exactly what the argument was, though she'd heard it enough from her friends lately. Something about broadening her horizons. Something about reigniting her womanly instincts. She looked at Connor as though she might read the words in his eyes, but they just weren't there.

"So who talked you into that fiasco tonight?" he asked her.

She frowned at him. "It was a blind date."

"No kidding. Even *you* wouldn't be nutty enough to go out with that guy voluntarily."

"Even me?" His words stung. What did he

think of her, anyway? Her eyes flashed. "Just how nutty am I, Connor?"

He reached out and grabbed her hand, gazing at her earnestly. "Will you stop? Please?"

She glanced back, her bottom lip trembling. Deep breaths. That was what she needed. And no matter what, she wasn't going to cry.

"So where have you been all this time?" she asked, wishing it didn't sound quite so petulant.

"All what time?" he said evasively.

"The year and a half since I last saw you."

Her gaze met his and skittered away again. She knew he was thinking about exactly what she was thinking about—that last time had been the day Brad left her. Neither one of them wanted to remember that day, much less talk about it. She grimaced and played with her spoon. The waitress brought their order so it was a moment or two before they spoke again.

"So you said your business is doing okay?" he noted as he spread his napkin on his lap.

"Yes." She stared down at the small dish of

ice cream she'd ordered and realized she wasn't going to be able to eat any of it. Her throat felt raw and tight. Too bad. It looked creamy and delicious.

He nodded, reaching for a fork. It was pretty clear he wasn't going to have any problem at all. "What business?"

She blinked at him. "Didn't you know? Didn't Brad tell you?"

He shook his head and avoided saying anything about Brad.

She waited a moment, then sighed. "Okay. When Brad left, he took the electronics business we had developed together. And told me I might as well go out and get a job once the babies were born."

He cringed. That was enough to set your teeth on edge, no matter who you were.

She met his gaze with a touch of defiance in her own. "But I gave birth to two little boys and looked at them and knew there was no way I was handing them over to someone else to raise for me. So I racked my brain, trying to find something I could do at home and still take care of them."

He nodded. That seemed the resourceful thing to do. Good for her. "So what did you decide on?"

She shrugged. "The only thing I was ever really good at. I started a Bundt Cake Bakery."

He nodded, waiting. There had to be more. Who could make a living baking Bundt cakes? "And?"

"And that's what I'm doing."

"Oh." He frowned, puzzled. "Great."

"It *is* great," she said defensively. She could hear the skepticism in his voice. "It was touch and go for a long time, but now I think I'm finally hitting my stride."

He nodded again, wishing he could rustle up some enthusiasm, but failing on all fronts. "Okay."

The product Jill and Brad had developed together had been a bit different from baked goods and he was having a hard time understanding the connection. Jill had done the bookkeeping and the marketing for the business. Brad had been the electronic genius. And Connor had done some work with them, too. They'd been successful from the first.

With that kind of background, he couldn't imagine how the profits from cakes could compare to what they'd made on the GPS device for hikers to be used as a map App. It had been new and fresh and sold very well. He wasn't sure what he could say.

He looked up across the restaurant, caught sight of someone coming in the door and he sighed. "You know how legend has it that everyone stops in at Rickey's on a Saturday night?"

Her eyes widened warily. "Sure."

"I guess it's true." He made a gesture with his head. "Look who just walked in. Mr. Mambo himself."

She gasped and whirled in her seat. Sure enough, there was Karl starting in their direction. He was coming through the restaurant as though he thought he owned the place, giving all the girls the eye. He caught sight of her and his eyes lit up.

Her heart fell. "Oh, no!"

CHAPTER TWO

AND THEN, KARL'S jaunty gaze fell on Connor and he stopped dead, visibly paling. Shaking his head, he raised his hands and he seemed to be muttering, "no, no," over and over again, as though to tell Connor he really didn't mean it. Turning on his heel, he left so quickly, Jill could almost believe she'd been imagining things.

"Wow." She turned back slowly and looked at Connor accusingly. "I guess he believed your cockeyed story." She put a hand to her forehead as though tragedy had struck. "Once he spreads the word, my dating days are done."

"Good," Connor said, beginning to attack his huge piece of cherry pie à la mode. "No point wasting your time on losers like that."

She made a face and leaned toward him sadly. "Are they all like that? Is it really hopeless?"

"Yes." He smiled at her. "Erase all thoughts of other men. I'm here. You don't need anybody else."

"Right." She rolled her eyes, knowing he was teasing. "You'd think I would have learned my lesson with Brad, wouldn't you?"

There was a catch in her voice as she said it. He looked up quickly and she knew he was afraid she might cry. But she didn't cry about that anymore. She was all cried out long ago on that subject.

Did he remember what a fool she'd been? How even with all the evidence piling up in her daily life, she'd never seen it coming. At the time she was almost eight months pregnant with the twins and having a hard time even walking, much less with thinking straight. And Connor had come to tell her that Brad was leaving her.

Brad had sent him, of course. The jerk couldn't even manage to face her and tell her himself.

That made her think twice. Here was Connor, back again. What was Brad afraid to tell her now?

She watched him, frowning, studying his blue eyes. Did she really want to know? All those months, all the heartbreak. Still, if it was something she needed to deal with, better get it over with. She took a deep breath and tried to sound strong and cool.

"So what does he want this time?"

Connor's head jerked back as though what she was asking was out of line. He waved his fork at her. "Do you think we could first go through some of the niceties our society has set up for situations like this?" he asked her.

She searched his face to see if he was mocking her, but he really wasn't. He was just uncomfortable.

"How about, 'How have you been?' or 'What have you been up to lately?' Why not give me some of the details of your life these days. Do we have to jump right into contentious things so quickly?"

So it wasn't good. She should have known. "You're the messenger, not me."

His handsome face winced. It almost seemed as though this pained him more than it was going to pain her. Fat chance.

"We're friends, aren't we?" he asked her.

Were they? She used to think so. "Sure. We always have been."

"So…"

He looked relieved, as though that made it all okay. But it wasn't okay. Whatever it was, it was going to hurt. She knew that instinctively. She leaned forward and glared at him.

"But you're on his side. Don't deny it."

He shook his head, denying it anyway. "What makes you say that?"

She shrugged. "That day, the one that ended life as I knew it, you came over to deliver the fatal blow. You set me straight as to how things really were." Her voice hardened. "You were the one who explained Brad to me at the time. You broke my heart and then you left me lying there in the dirt and you never came back."

"You were not lying in the dirt." He seemed outraged at the concept.

She closed her eyes and then opened them again. "It's a metaphor, silly."

"I don't care what it is. I did not leave you lying in the dirt or even in the sand, or on the couch, or anything. You were standing straight and tall and making jokes, just like always."

Taking a deep breath, he forced himself to relax a bit. "You seemed calm and collected and fine with it. Like you'd known it was coming. Like you were prepared. Sad, but okay." He shook his head, willing her to believe what he was saying. "Or else I never would have left you alone."

She shrugged carelessly. How could he have gotten it all so wrong? "And you think you know me."

He pushed away the pie, searching her eyes,

looking truly distressed. "Sara was with you. Your sister. I thought…"

He looked away, frowning fiercely. He remembered what he'd thought. He'd seen the pain in her face and it had taken everything in him not to reach out and gather her in his arms and kiss her until she realized…until she knew… No, he'd had to get out of there before he did something stupid. And that was why he left her. He had his own private hell to tend to.

"You thought I was okay? Wow." She struck a pose and put on an accent. "The corpse was bleeding profusely, but I assumed it would stop on its own. She seemed to be coping quite well with her murder."

He grimaced, shaking his head.

"I hated you for a while," she admitted. "It was easier than hating Brad. What Brad had done to me was just too confusing. What you did was common, everyday cowardice."

He stared at her, aghast. "Oh, thanks."

"And to make it worse, you never did come back. Did you?"

He shook his head as though he really couldn't understand why she was angry. He hadn't done anything to make her that way. He'd just lived his life like he always did, following the latest impulse that moved him. Didn't she know that?

"I was gone. I left the country. I…I had a friend starting up a business in Singapore, so I went to help him out."

She looked skeptical and deep, deep down, she looked hurt. "All this time?"

"Yeah." He nodded, feeling a bit defensive. "I've been out of the country all this time."

Funny, but that made her feel a lot better. At least he hadn't been coming up here to Seattle and never contacting her.

"So you haven't been to see Brad?"

He hesitated. He couldn't lie to her. "I stopped in to see Brad in Portland last week," he admitted.

She threw up her hands. "See? You're on his side."

He wanted to growl at her. "I'm not on anybody's side. I've been friends with both of you since that first week of college, when we all three camped out in Brad's car together."

The corners of Jill's mouth quirked into a reluctant smile as she remembered. "What a night that was," she said lightly. "They'd lost my housing forms and you hadn't been admitted yet. We had no place to sleep."

"So Brad offered his car."

"And stayed out with us."

"We talked and laughed the whole night."

She nodded, remembering. "And that cemented it. We were best buds from that night on."

Connor smiled, but looked away. He remembered meeting Jill in the administration office while they both tried to fight the bureaucracy. He'd thought she was the cutest coed on campus, right from the start. And then Brad showed up and swept her off her feet.

"We fought the law and the law won," he noted cynically.

"Right." She laughed softly, still remembering. "You with that crazy book of rules you were always studying on how to make professors fall in love with you so they'd give you good grades."

He sighed. "That never worked. And it should have, darn it all."

Her eyes narrowed as she looked back into the past a little deeper. "And all those insane jobs you took, trying to pay off your fees. I never understood when you had time to study."

"I slept with a tape recorder going," he said with a casual shrug. "Subliminal learning. Without it, I would have flunked out early on."

She stared at him, willing him to smile and admit he'd made that up, but he stuck to his guns.

"No, really. I learned French that way."

She gave him an incredulous look. *"Parlez-vous francais?"*

"Uh…whatever." He looked uncomfortable. "I didn't say I retained any of it beyond test day."

"Right." She laughed at him and he grinned back.

But she knew they were ignoring the elephant in the room. Brad. Brad who had been with them both all through college. Brad who had decided she was his from the start. And what Brad wanted, Brad usually got. She'd been flattered by his attention, then thrilled with it. And soon, she'd fallen hard. She was so in love with him, she knew he was her destiny. She let him take over her life. She didn't realize he would toss it aside when he got tired of it.

"So what are you doing here?" she asked again. "Surely you didn't come to see me."

"Jill, I always want to see you."

"No kidding. That's why you've been gone for a year and a half. You've never even met the twins."

He looked at her with a half smile. Funny. She'd been pregnant the last time he'd seen her, but that wasn't the way he'd thought of her all these months. And to tell the truth, Brad had never mentioned those babies. "That's right. I forgot. You've got a couple of cookie crunchers now, don't you?"

"I do. The little lights of my life, so to speak."

"Boys."

"Boys." She nodded.

He wanted to ask how they got along with Brad, but he wasn't brave enough to do it. Besides, it was getting late. She had a pair of baby boys at home. She looked at her watch, then looked at him.

"I've got to get home. If you can just drop me at the dock, the last ferry goes at midnight and..."

He waved away her suggestion. "You will not walk home from the ferry landing. It's too late and too far."

She made a face. "I'll be fine. I've done it a thousand times."

"I'll drive you."

She gave him a mock glare. "Well, then we'd better get going or you won't make the last ferry back."

"You let me worry about that."

Let him worry—let him manage—leave it to him. Something inside her yearned to be able to do that. It had been so long since she'd had anyone else to rely on. But life had taught her a hard lesson. If you relied on others, they could really hurt you. Best to rely on nobody but yourself.

The ferry ride across the bay to the island was always fun. He pulled the car into the proper space on the ferry and they both got out to enjoy the trip. Standing side by side as the ferry started off, they watched the inky-black water part to let them through.

Jill pulled her arms in close, fending off the

ocean coolness, and he reached out and put an arm around her, keeping her warm. She rested her head on his shoulder. He had to resist the urge to draw her closer.

"Hey, I'm looking forward to meeting those two little boys of yours," he said.

"Hopefully you won't meet them tonight," she said, laughing. "I've got a nice older lady looking after them. They should be sound asleep right now."

"It's amazing to think of you with children," he said.

She nodded. "I know. You're not the only one stunned by the transformation." She smiled, thinking of how they really had changed her life. If only Brad... No, she wasn't going to start going back over those old saws again. That way lay madness.

"It's also amazing to think of how long we've known each other," she added brightly instead.

"We all three got close in our freshman year," he agreed, "and that lasted all through college."

She nodded. "It seemed, those first couple of years, we did everything together."

"I remember it well." He sighed and glanced down at her. All he could see was that mop of crazy, curly blond hair. It always made him smile. "You were sighing over Brad," he added to the memory trail. "And I was wishing you would look my way instead."

She looked up and made a face at him. "Be serious. You had no time for stodgy, conventional girls like I was. You were always after the high flyers."

He stared at her, offended despite the fact that there was some truth in what she said. "I was not," he protested anyway.

"Sure you were." She was teasing him now. "You liked bad girls. Edgy girls. The ones who ran off with the band."

His faint smile admitted the truth. "Only when I was in the band."

"And that was most of the time." She pulled

back and looked at him. "Did you ever actually get a degree?"

"Of course I got a degree."

She giggled. "In what? Multicultural dating?"

He bit back the sharp retort that surfaced in his throat. She really didn't know. But why should she? He had to admit he'd spent years working hard at seeming to be a slacker.

"Something like that," he muttered, thinking with a touch of annoyance about his engineering degree with a magna cum laude attached. No one had been closer friends to him than Brad and Jill. And they didn't even realize he was smarter than he seemed.

It was his own fault of course. He'd worked on that easygoing image. Still, it stung a bit.

And it made him do a bit of "what if?" thinking. What if he'd been more aggressive making his own case? What if he'd challenged Brad's place in Jill's heart at the time? What if he'd competed instead of accepting their romance as an established fact? Would things have been different?

The spray from the water splashed across his face, jerking him awake from his dream. Turning toward the island, he could see her house up the drive a block from the landing. He'd been there a hundred times before, but not for quite a while. Not since the twins were born and Brad decided he wasn't fatherhood material. Connor had listened to what Brad had to say and it had caused a major conflict for him. He thought Brad's reasons were hateful and he deplored them, but at the same time, he'd seen them together for too long to have any illusions. They didn't belong together. Getting a divorce was probably the best thing Brad could do for Jill. So he'd gone with his message, he'd done his part and hated it and then he'd headed for Singapore.

He turned to look at her, to watch the way the wind blew her hair over her eyes, and that old familiar pull began somewhere in the middle of his chest. It started slow and then began to build, as though it was slowly finding its way through his bloodstream. He wanted her, wanted to hold her and kiss her and tell her.... He gritted his teeth and turned away. He had to fight that feeling. Funny. He never got it with any other girl. It only happened with her. Damn.

A flash of panic shivered through him. What the hell was he doing here, anyway? He'd thought he was prepared for this. Hardened. Toughened and ready to avoid the tender trap that was always Jill. But his defenses were fading fast. He had to get out of here.

He needed a plan. Obviously playing this by ear wasn't going to work. The first thing he had to do was to get her home, safe and sound. That should be easy. Then he had to avoid getting out of the car. Under no circumstances should he go into the house, especially not to take a peek at the babies. That would tie him up in a web of sentiment and leave him raw and vulnerable to his feelings. He couldn't afford to do that. At all costs, he had to stay strong and leave right away.

He could come back and talk to her in the morning. If he hung around, disaster was inevitable. He couldn't let that happen.

"You know what?" he said, trying to sound light and casual. "I think you really had the right idea about this. I need to get back to the hotel. I think I'll take the ferry right on back and let you walk up the hill on your own. It's super safe here, isn't it? I mean..."

He felt bad about it, but it had to be done. He couldn't go home with her. Wouldn't be prudent, as someone once had famously said.

But he realized she wasn't listening to him. She was staring, mouth open, over his shoulder at the island they were fast approaching.

"What in the world is going on? My house is lit up like a Christmas tree."

He turned. She was right. Every window was ablaze with light. It was almost midnight. Somehow, this didn't seem right.

And then a strange thing happened. As they watched, something came flying out of the upstairs window, sailed through the air and landed on the roof next door.

Jill gasped, rigid with shock. "Was that the cat?" she cried. "Oh, my God!"

She tried to pull away from him as though she was about to jump into the water and swim for shore, but he yanked her back. "Come on," he said urgently, pulling her toward the Camaro. "We'll get there faster in the car."

CHAPTER THREE

Jill's heart was racing. She couldn't think. She could hardly breathe. Adrenaline surged and she almost blacked out with it.

"Oh, please," she muttered over and over as they raced toward the house. "Oh, please, oh, please!"

He swung the car into the driveway and she jumped out before he even came to a stop, running for the door.

"Timmy?" she called out. "Tanner?"

Connor was right behind her as she threw open the front door and raced inside.

"Mrs. Mulberry?" she called out as she ran. "Mrs. Mulberry!"

A slight, gray-haired woman appeared on the stairway from the second floor with a look close to terror on her face. "Oh, thank God you're finally here! I tried to call you but my hands were shaking so hard, I couldn't use the cell phone."

"What is it?" Jill grabbed her by the shoulders, staring down into her face. "What's happened? Where are the boys?"

"I tried, I really tried, but…but…"

"Mrs. Mulberry! What?"

Her face crumpled and she wailed, "They locked me out. I couldn't get to them. I didn't know what to do.…"

"What do you mean they've locked you out? Where? When?"

"They got out of their cribs and locked the door. I couldn't…"

Jill started up the stairs, but Connor took them two at a time and beat her to the landing and then the door. He yanked at the handle but it didn't budge.

"Timmy? Tanner? Are you okay?" Jill's voice quavered as she pressed her ear to the door. There was no response.

"There's a key," she said, turning wildly, trying to remember where she'd put it. "I know there's a key."

Connor pushed her aside. "No time," he said, giving the door a wicked kick right next to where the lever sat. There was a crunch of wood breaking and the door flew open.

A scene of chaos and destruction was revealed. A lamp was upside down on the floor, along with pillows and books and a tumbled table and chair set. Toys were everywhere, most of them covered with baby powder that someone had been squirting out of the container. And on the other side of the room were two little blond boys, crowding into a window they could barely reach. They saw the adults coming for them, looked at each other and shrieked—and then they very quickly shoved one fat fluffy pillow and then one large plastic game of Hungry Hungry Hippos over the sill. The hippos could be heard hitting the bricks of the patio below.

"What are you doing?" Jill cried, dashing in as one child reached for a small music toy. She grabbed him, swung him up in her arms and held him close.

"You are such a bad boy!" she said, but she was laughing with relief at the same time. They seemed to be okay. No broken bones. No blood. No dead cat.

Connor pulled up the other boy with one arm while he slammed the window shut with the other. He looked at Jill and shook his head. "Wow," was all he could say. Then he thought of something else. "Oh. Sorry about the door. I thought…"

"You thought right," she said, flashing him a look of pure relief and happiness. Her babies were safe and right now that was all that mattered to her. "I would have had a heart attack if I'd had to wait any longer."

Mrs. Mulberry was blubbering behind them and they both turned, each carrying a child, to stare at her.

"I'm so sorry," she was saying tearfully. "But when they locked me out…"

"Okay, start at the beginning," Jill told her, trying to keep her temper in check and hush her baby, who was saying, "Mamamama" over and over in her ear. "What exactly happened?"

The older woman sniffled and put a handkerchief to her nose. "I…I don't really know. It all began so well. They were perfect angels."

She smiled at them tearfully and they grinned back at her. Jill shook her head. It was as though they knew exactly what they'd done and were ready to do it again if they got the chance.

"They were so good," Mrs. Mulberry was saying, "I'm afraid I let them stay up longer than I should have. Finally I put them to bed and went downstairs." She shook her head as though she still couldn't believe what happened next. "I was reading a magazine on the couch when something just went plummeting by the bay window. I thought it was my imagination at first. Then something else went shooting past and I got up and went outside to look at what was going on. And there were toys and bits of bedding just lying there in the grass. I looked up but I couldn't see anything. It was very eerie. Almost scary. I couldn't figure out what on earth was happening."

"Oh, sweetie boys," Jill muttered, holding one closely to her. "You must be good for the baby-sitter. Remember?"

"When I started to go back in the house," the older lady went on, "one of these very same adorable children was at the front door. As I started to come closer, he grinned at me and he…" She had to stop to take a shaky breath. "He just smiled. I realized what might happen and I called out. I said, 'No! Wait!' But just as I reached the door, he slammed it shut. It was locked. He locked me out of the house!"

Jill was frowning. "What are you talking about? Who locked you out of the house?"

She pointed at Timmy who was cuddled close in Jill's arms. "He did."

Jill shook her head as though to clear it. He's

only eighteen months old. "That's impossible. He doesn't know how to lock doors."

Mrs. Mulberry drew herself up. "Oh, yes he does," she insisted.

Jill looked into Timmy's innocent face. Could her baby have done that? He smiled and said, "Mamamama." No way.

"I couldn't get in," Mrs Mulberry went on. "I was panicking. I didn't know what I was going to do." Tears filled her eyes again.

Jill stared at her in disbelief and Connor stepped forward, putting a comforting hand on her shoulder. "We believe you, Mrs. Mulberry," he said calmly. "Just finish your story. We want to know it all."

She tried to give him a grateful smile and went on. "I was racing around, trying all the doors, getting more and more insane with fear. Finally I got the idea to look for a key. I must have turned over twenty flower pots before I found it. Once I got back into the house, I realized they were up here in the bedroom, but when I called to them, they locked the bedroom door."

She sighed heavily, her head falling forward on her chest. "I thought I would go out of my mind. I tried to call you but I couldn't do it. I thought I ought to call the police, but I was shaking so badly..." She shuddered, remembering. "And then you finally came home."

Jill met Connor's gaze and bit her lip, turning to lay Timmy down in his crib. He was giving her a warning glance, as if to say, "No major damage here. Give her a break."

For some reason, instead of letting it annoy her, she felt a surge of relief. Yes, give her a break. Dear soul, she didn't mean any harm, and since nothing had really happened, there was no reason to make things worse. In fact, both boys were already drifting off to sleep. And why not? They'd had a busy night so far.

Turning, she smiled at the older woman. "Thank goodness I got back when I did," she said as lightly as she could manage. "Well, everything's alright now. If you'll wait downstairs, I'll just put these two down and…"

Connor gave her a grin and a wink and put down the already sleeping Tanner into his crib as though he knew what he was doing, which surprised her. But her mind was on her babies, and she looked down lovingly at them as they slept. For just a moment, she'd been so scared….

What would she do if anything happened to either one of them? She couldn't let herself think about that. That was a place she didn't want to go.

Connor watched her. He was pretty sure he knew what she was thinking about. Anything happening to her kids would just about destroy her. He'd seen her face when she first realized she was losing Brad. He remembered that pain almost as if it had been his own. And losing these little ones would be ten times worse.

He drove Mrs. Mulberry home and when he got back, all was quiet. The lights that had blazed out across the landscape were doused and a more muted atmosphere prevailed. The house seemed to be at peace.

Except for one thing—the sound of sniffles coming from the kitchen where Jill was sitting at the table with her hands wrapped around a cup of coffee.

"Hey," he said, sliding in beside her on the bench seat. "You okay?"

She turned her huge, dark, tragic eyes toward him.

"I leave the house for just a few hours— leave the boys for more than ten minutes—the first time in a year. And chaos takes over." She searched his gaze for answers. "Is that really not allowed? Am I chained to this place, this life, forever? Do I not dare leave…ever?"

He stared down at her. He wanted to make a joke, make her smile, get her out of this mood, but he saw real desperation in her eyes and he couldn't make light of that.

"Hey." He brushed her cheek with the backs of his fingers. "It's not forever. Things change quickly for kids. Don't let it get you down. In a month, it will be different."

She stared up at him. How could he possibly know that? And yet, somehow, she saw the wisdom in what he'd said. She shook her head and smiled. "Connor, why didn't you come back sooner? I love your smile."

He gave her another one, but deep down, he groaned. This was exactly why he had to get out of here as soon as he could. He slumped down lower in the seat and tried to think of something else reassuring to say, but his mind wouldn't let go of what she'd just said to him.

I love your smile.

Pretty pathetic to grasp at such a slender reed, but that was just about all he had, wasn't it?

Jill was back on the subject at hand, thinking about the babysitter. "Here I hired her because I thought an older woman would be calmer with a steadier hand." She rolled her eyes. "A teenage girl would have been better."

"Come on, that's not really fair. She got a lot

thrown at her at once and she wasn't prepared for it. It could have happened to anyone."

She shook her head as though she just couldn't accept that. "I'm lucky I've got my sister close by for emergencies. But she's getting more and more caught up in her career, and it's a pretty demanding one. I really can't count on her for too much longer." She sighed. "She had to be at a business dinner in Seattle tonight, or she would have been here to take care of the boys."

"Family can be convenient." He frowned. "Don't you have a younger sister? I thought I met her once."

Instead of answering, she moaned softly and closed her eyes. "Kelly. Yes. She was our half sister." She looked at him, new tragedy clouding her gaze. "Funny you should remember her tonight. She was killed in a car crash last week."

"Oh, my God. Oh, Jill, I'm so sorry."

She nodded. "It's sad and tragic and brings on a lot of guilty feelings for Sara and me."

He shook his head, not understanding. "What did you have to do with it?"

"The accident? Oh, nothing. It happened in Virginia where I guess she was living lately. The guilt comes from not even knowing exactly where she was and frankly, not thinking about her much. We should have paid more attention and worked a little harder on being real sisters to her."

There was more. He could tell. But he waited, letting her take her time to unravel the story.

"She was a lot younger, of course. Our mother died when we were pretty young, and our father remarried soon after. Too soon for us, of course. After losing our mother, we couldn't bear to share our beloved father with anyone. We resented the new woman, and when she had a baby, we pretty much resented her, too." She shook her head. "It was so unfair. Poor little girl."

"Didn't you get closer as she got older?"

"Not really. You see, the marriage was a disaster from the start and it ended by the time Kelly was about five years old. We only saw her occasionally after that, for a few hours at a time. And then our father died by the time she was fifteen and we didn't see either one of them much at all after that."

"That's too bad."

She nodded. "Yes. I'm really sorry about it now." She sighed. "She was something of a wild child, at least according to my father's tales of woe. Getting into trouble even in high school. The sort of girl who wants to test the boundaries and explore the edge."

"I know your father died a few years ago. What about your stepmother?"

"She died when I was about twenty-three. She had cancer."

"Poor lady."

"Yes. Just tragic, isn't it? Lives snuffed out so casually." She shook her head. "I just feel so bad about Kelly. It's so sad that we never got to know her better."

"Just goes to show. Carpe diem. Seize the day. Don't let your opportunities slip by."

"Yes." She gave him a look. "When did you become such a philosopher?"

"I've always been considered wise among my peers," he told her in a snooty voice that made her laugh.

A foghorn sounded its mournful call and she looked up at a clock. "And now here you are, stuck. The last ferry's gone. You're going to have to stay here."

He smiled at her. "Unless I hijack a boat."

"You can sleep on the couch." She shrugged. "Or sleep in the master bedroom if you want. Nobody else does."

The bitter tone was loud and clear, and it surprised him.

"Where do you sleep?" he asked her.

"In the guest room." Her smile was bittersweet. "That's why you can't use it."

He remembered glancing in at the master bedroom when he was upstairs. It looked like it had always looked. She and Brad had shared that bed. He looked back at her and didn't say a word.

She didn't offer an explanation, but he knew what it was. She couldn't sleep in that bed now that Brad had abandoned it.

He nodded. "I'll take the couch."

She hesitated. "The only problem with that is, I'll be getting up about four in the morning. I'll probably wake you."

"Four in the morning? Planning a rendezvous with the milkman?"

"No, silly. I've got to start warming the ovens and mixing my batter." She yawned, reminding him of a sleepy kitten. "I've got a day full of large orders to fill tomorrow. One of my busiest days ever." She smiled again. "And hopefully, a sign of success. I sure need it."

"Great."

"Wait here a second. I think I've got some-thing you can use."

She left the room and was back in moments, carrying a set of dark blue men's pajamas.

He recoiled at the sight. "Brad's?" he said.

"Not really." She threw them down in his lap. "I bought them for Brad but he never even saw them. That was just days before he sent you to tell me we were through."

"Oh." That was okay, then. He looked at them, setting aside the top and reserving the pants for when he was ready for bed. Meanwhile, she was rummaging through a linen closet and bringing out a sheet and a light blanket. That made her look domestic in ways he hadn't remembered. He thought about how she'd looked with Timmy in her arms.

"Hey," he said gently. "That's a pair of great little boys you've got there."

She melted immediately. "Aren't they adorable? But so bad!"

"I'll bet they keep you busy every hour of the day."

She nodded. "It's not easy running a busi-

ness from home when I've got those two getting more and more mischievous." She sighed
and sat back down. "Can you believe they were
locking doors? I had no idea they knew what a
lock was."

"Time to dismantle some and add extra keys
for others," he suggested.

"Yes. And keep my eyes on them every minute."

"Can't you hire a daytime babysitter?"

"Yeah, hiring a babysitter really works out
well, doesn't it?" She shook her head. "Actually Trini, my bakery assistant, helps a lot. She
doubles as a babysitter when I need her to, and
does everything else the rest of the time. And
then, Sara comes by and helps when she has a
free moment or two." She gave him a tremulous
smile. "We manage."

He resisted the impulse to reach out and brush
back the lock of hair that was bouncing over her
eyebrow. The gesture seemed a little too inti-

mate as they sat here, alone in the dim light so late at night.

But Jill didn't seem to have the same reservations he harbored. She reached out and took his hand in hers, startling him. Then she gazed deep into his eyes for a moment before she spoke. His pulse began to quicken. He wasn't sure what she wanted from him, but he knew he couldn't deny her much.

"Well?" she said softly.

He could barely breathe. His fingers curled around hers and he looked at her full, soft lips, her warm mouth, and he wanted to kiss her so badly his whole body ached with it. The longing for her seared his soul. What would she do if he just...?

"Well?" she said again. "Out with it."

"What?" His brain was fuzzy. He couldn't connect what she was saying to what he was feeling.

"Come on. Say it."

He shook his head. What was she talking

about? Her brows drew together and her gaze was more penetrating.

"My dear Connor," she said, pulling at his hand as though to make him say what she wanted to hear. "It is time for you to come clean."

"Come clean?"

He swallowed hard. Did she know? Could she read the desire in his eyes? Did she see how he felt about her in his face? Hear it in his voice? Had he really let his guard down too far?

"On what?" he added, his voice gruff with suppressed emotion.

"On why you're here." She was looking so intense. "On why Brad sent you." She searched his eyes again. "Come on, Connor. What exactly does he want this time?"

Brad. His heart sank, and then he had to laugh at himself. Of course that was what she was thinking about. And why not? What right did he have to want anything different? What he wanted didn't mean a thing. This was all about

Jill—and Brad. As usual. He took a deep breath and shook his head.

"What makes you think Brad sent me?" he said, his voice coming out a bit harsher than he'd meant it to.

"You're his best friend." She frowned and looked pensive. "You were my best friend once, too."

There you go. Too many best friends. He was always the odd man out. That was exactly why he'd opted for Singapore when he had the chance. And maybe why he would go back again.

He raised her hand and brought it to his lips, touching her gently with a kiss, then setting her aside and drawing away.

"Jill, you've had enough excitement for to-night. Let's talk in the morning."

"No, tell me. What does Brad want me to do?"

It was the question in her eyes that scared him—the hint of hope. She didn't really think that there was a chance that Brad might want her back….did she? It wasn't going to happen. He'd seen it with his own eyes.

Brad was a selfish bastard. It had taken him years to accept that. Maybe Jill didn't realize it yet. Brad was a great guy to hang out with. Playing poker with him was fun. Going water-skiing. Box seats at a Mariners game. But as far as planning your life with him, he wouldn't recommend it.

"Jill, I didn't come for Brad. I came to see you because I wanted to come."

Okay, so that was partly a lie. But he had to say it. He couldn't stand to see the glimmer of hope in her eyes, knowing it would only bring her more heartbreak. He had a message from Brad all right. But right now, he wasn't sure if he would ever tell her what it was. She thought he was on Brad's side, but she was wrong. If it came to a showdown, he was here for her—all the way.

He just wasn't sure how much she cared, one way or the other. She still wanted Brad. He could see it in her face, hear it in her voice. He shouldn't even be here.

No worries. He would leave first thing in the morning. He couldn't leave before six when the ferry started to run, but he would slip out while she was busy. No goodbyes. Just leave. Get it over with and out of the way and move on. That was the plan. He only had to follow it.

The couch was comfortable enough but he could only sleep in short snatches. When he did doze off, he had dreams that left him wandering through crowds of Latin American dancers in huge headdresses, all swaying wildly to exotic music and shouting "Mambo!" in his face.

He was looking for something he couldn't find. People kept getting in his way, trying to get him to dance with them. And then one headdress changed into a huge white parrot before his eyes, the most elegant bird he'd ever seen. He had to catch that parrot. Suddenly it was an obvious case of life or death and his heart was beating hard with the effort as he chased it through the crowd. He had to catch it!

He reached out, leaped high and touched the tips of the white feathers of its wings. His heart soared. He had it! But then the feathers slipped through his fingers and the bird was swooping away from him. He was left with nothing. A feeling of cold, dark devastation filled his heart. He began to walk away.

But the parrot was back, trailing those long white fathers across his face—only it wasn't white feathers. It was the sleeve of a lacy white nightgown and it was Jill leaning over him, trying to reach something from the bookcase behind the couch.

"Oh, sorry. I didn't want to wake you up," she whispered as though he might go back to sleep if she was quiet about it. "It's not time to get up. I just needed this manual. I'm starting to heat the ovens up."

He nodded and pretended to close his eyes, but he left slits so he could watch her make her way across the room, her lacy white gown cascading around her gorgeous ankles. The glow from the kitchen provided a backlight that showed off her curves to perfection, making his body tighten in a massive way he didn't expect.

And then he fell into the first real deep and dreamless sleep of the night. It must have lasted at least two hours. When he opened his eyes, he found himself staring into the bright blue gaze of one of the twins. He didn't know which one. He couldn't tell them apart yet.

He closed his eyes again, hoping the little visitor would be gone when he opened them. No such luck. Now there were two of them, both dressed in pajamas, both cute as could be.

"Hi," he said. "How are you doing?"

They didn't say a word. They just stared harder. But maybe they didn't do much talking at this age. They were fairly young.

Still, this soundless staring was beginning to get on his nerves.

"Boo," he said.

They both blinked but held their ground.

"So it's going to take more than a simple 'boo,' is it?" he asked.

They stared.

"Okay." He gathered his forces and sprang up, waving the covers like a huge cloak around him. "BOO!" he yelled, eyes wide.

They reacted nicely. They both ran screaming from the room, tumbling over each other in their hurry, and Connor smiled with satisfaction.

It only took seconds for Jill to arrive around the corner.

"What are you doing to my babies?" she cried.

"Nothing," he said, trying to look innocent. He wrapped the covers around himself and smiled. "Just getting to know them. Establishing pecking order. Stuff like that."

She frowned at him suspiciously. To his disappointment, she didn't have the lacy white thing on anymore. She'd changed into a crisp uniform with a large apron and wore a net over her mass of curly hair.

He gestured in her direction. "Regulation uniform, huh?"

She nodded. "I'm a Bundt cake professional, you know," she reminded him, doing a pose.

Then she smiled, looking him over. "You look cute when you're sleepy," she told him, reaching out to ruffle his badly mussed hair. "Why don't you go take a shower? I put fresh towels in the downstairs bathroom. I'll give you some breakfast before you leave."

Leave? Leave? Oh, yeah. He was going to leave as fast as he could. That was the plan.

He let the sheet drop, forgetting that his torso was completely naked, but the look on her face reminded him quickly. "Oh, sorry," he said, pulling the sheet back. And then he felt like a fool.

He glanced at her. A beautiful shade of crimson was flooding her face. That told him something he hadn't figured out before. But knowing she responded to him like that didn't help matters. In fact, it only made things worse. He swore softly to himself.

"You want me gone as soon as possible, don't you?" He shouldn't have said it that way, but the words were already out of his mouth.

She looked a little startled, but she nodded. "Actually you are sort of in the way," she noted a bit breathlessly. "I…I've got a ton of work to do today and I don't really have time to be much of a hostess."

He nodded. "Don't worry. I'm on my way."

He thought about getting into his car and driving off and he wondered why he wasn't really looking forward to it. He had to go. He knew it. She knew it. It had to be done. They needed to stay away from each other if they didn't want to start something they might not be able to stop. Just the thought made his pulse beat a ragged rhythm.

She met his gaze and looked almost sorry for

a moment, then took a deep breath, shook her head and glanced at her watch.

"So far, so good. I'm pretty much on schedule," she said. "It can get wild around here. My assistant, Trini, should show up about seven. Then things will slowly get under control."

Despite her involuntary reaction to seeing him without a shirt—a reaction that sent a surge through his bloodstream every time he thought of it—there was still plenty of tension in her voice. Best to be gone before he really felt like a burden. He shook his head as he went off to take a shower.

It can get wild around here, she'd said. So it seemed. It couldn't get much wilder than it had the night before.

That reminded him of what those boys were capable of, and once he'd finished his shower, he took a large plastic bag and went outside to collect all the items the boys had thrown down from the bedroom. Then he brought the plastic bag into the house and set it down in the entryway.

"Oh, good," Jill said when she saw what he'd done. She looked relieved that he'd changed back into the shirt and slacks he'd been wearing the night before. "I forgot. I really did want all the stuff brought in before the neighbors saw it."

"This is quite a haul," he told her with a crooked smile. "Are you sure your guys aren't in training to be second-story men?"

"Very funny," she said, shaking her head at him, then smiling back. "There are actually times when I wonder how I'm going to do it on my own. Raise them right, I mean." She turned large, sad eyes his way. "It's not getting any easier."

It broke his heart to see her like this. If only there was something he could do to help her. But that was impossible, considering the situation. If it weren't for Brad… But that was just wishful thinking.

"You're going to manage it," he reassured her.

"You've got what it takes. You'll do it just like your parents managed to raise you. It comes with the territory."

She was frowning at him. "But it doesn't always work out. Your parents, for instance. Didn't you used to say...?"

He tried to remember what he'd ever told her about his childhood. He couldn't have said much. He never did. Unless he'd had too much to drink one night and opened up to her. But he didn't remember anything like that. Where had she come up with the fact that his parents had been worthless? It was the truth, but he usually didn't advertise it.

"Yeah, you're right," he said slowly. "My parents were pretty much AWOL. But you know what? Kids usually grow up okay anyway." He spread his arms out and smiled at her. "Look at me."

"Just about perfect," she teased. "Who could ask for anything more?"

"My point exactly," he said.

She turned away. She knew he was trying to give her encouragement, but what he was saying was just so much empty talk. It wouldn't get her far.

"Come on," she said. "I've got coffee, and as long as you want cake for breakfast, you can eat."

The cake was slices from rejects—Dutch Apple Crust, Lemon Delight and Double Devil's Food—but they were great and she knew it. She watched with satisfaction as he ate four slices in a row, making happy noises all the while.

The boys were playing in the next room. They were making plenty of noise but none of it sounded dangerous so far. Her batters were mixed. Her first cakes were baking. She still had to prepare some glazes. But all in all, things were moving along briskly and she was feeling more confident.

A moment of peace. She slipped into a chair and smiled across the table at him.

"You look like a woman expecting a busy

day," he noted, smiling back at her and noticing how the morning light set off the faint sprinkling of freckles that still decorated her pretty face.

She nodded. "It's my biggest day ever. I've got to get cakes to the charity auction at the Lodge, I've got cakes due for six parties, I've got a huge order, an engagement party at the country club today at three. They want 125 mini Bundt cakes. I was planning to get started on them last night, but after the baby riot, I just didn't have the energy." She shook her head. "As soon as Trini gets here, we'll push the 'on' switch and we won't turn it off until we're done."

He grinned at her. "You look like you relish the whole thing. Or am I reading you wrong?"

"You've got it right." She gave him a warm look. "I really appreciate you being here to help me last night," she said, shaking her head as she remembered the madness. "That was so crazy."

"Yeah," he agreed, polishing off the last piece

of Lemon Delight. "But nobody got hurt. It all turned out all right."

She nodded, looking at him, at his dark, curly hair, at his calm, honest face. She felt a surge of affection for him, and that made her frown. They'd been such good friends at one point, but she hardly knew anything about what he'd been doing lately. He'd walked out of her life at the same time Brad had. Both her best friends had deserted her in one way or another.

What doesn't kill you makes you stronger. Yeah, right.

"So the way I understand it," she said, leaning forward, "you've been in Singapore for the last year or so."

"That's right."

"Are you back for good?"

"Uh…" He grimaced. "Hard to say. I've got some options. Haven't decided what I want to do."

She thought about that for a moment. Did Connor ever have a solid plan? Or was it just that he kept his feelings close to the vest? She couldn't tell at this point. She resented the way he'd walked off over a year ago, but that didn't mean she didn't still love him to death.

Best friends. Right?

She narrowed her eyes, then asked brightly, "How about getting married?"

He looked at her as though she'd suddenly gone insane. "What? Married? Who to?"

She laughed. She could read his mind. He thought she was trying out a brand-new idea and he was ready to panic. "Not to me, silly. To someone you love. Someone who will enhance your life."

"Oh." He still looked uncomfortable.

"I'm serious. You should get married. You could use some stability in your life. A sense of purpose." She shrugged, feeling silly.

Who was she to give this sort of advice? Not only was she a failure at marriage, but she'd turned out to be a pretty lousy judge of character, too. "Someone to love," she added lamely.

His blue eyes were hooded as he gazed at her. "How do you know I don't have all those things right now?"

She studied his handsome face and shook her head. "I don't see it. To me, you look like the same old Connor, always chasing the next good time. Show me how I'm wrong."

She knew she was getting a little personal, but she was feeling a little confused about him right now. What was he doing here? Why was he sticking around?

In the bright light of day she thought she could see things more clearly, and that fresh sight told her he'd come with a goal in mind. If he'd just wanted to see her, make a visit, he'd have called ahead. No, Brad had sent him. Coming face-to-face in the hotel dining room had been a fluke. But what did Brad have in mind? Why didn't Connor just deliver the message and go?

She was beginning to feel annoyed with him. Actually she was becoming annoyed with everything. Something was off-kilter and her day was beginning to stretch out ominously before her.

"Okay, let's stop avoiding the real issue here." She stared at him coolly. "No more denials. What does Brad really want?"

CHAPTER FOUR

"Brad?"

Jill saw the shift in Connor's eyes. He didn't want to talk about this right now. He was perfectly ready to avoid the issue again. Well, too bad. She didn't have all the time in the world. It was now or never.

"Yes, Brad. You remember him. My ex-husband. The father of my children. The man who was once my entire life."

"Oh, yeah. That guy."

She frowned. He was still being evasive. She locked her fingers together and pulled.

"So, what does he want?" she insisted.

Connor looked at her and began to smile. "What do you think Brad wants? He always wants more than his share. And he usually gets it."

She shook her head, surprised, then laughed softly. "You do know him well, don't you?"

Connor's smile faded. He glanced around the kitchen, looking uncomfortable. "Does he have visitation rights to the boys? Does he come up here to see them or does he…?"

"No," she said quickly. "He's never seen them."

For once, she'd shocked him. His face showed it clearly. "Never seen his own kids? Why? Do you have a court injunction or…?"

The pain of it all would bring her down if she let it. She couldn't do that. She held her head high and met his gaze directly.

"He doesn't want to see them. Don't you know that? Didn't he ever tell you why he wanted the divorce?"

Connor shook his head slowly. "Tell me," he said softly.

She took a deep breath. "When Brad asked me to marry him, he told me he wanted a partner. He was going to start his own business and he wanted someone as committed to it as he was, someone who would stand by him and help him succeed. I entered into that project joyfully."

Connor nodded. He remembered that as well. He'd been there. He'd worked right along with them. They'd spent hours together brainstorming ideas, trying out options, failing and trying again. They'd camped out in sleeping bags when they first opened their office. They'd been so young and so naive. They thought they could change the world—or at least their little corner of it. They'd invented new ways of doing things and found a way to make it pay. It had been a lot of hard work, but they'd had a lot of fun along the way. That time seemed a million miles away now.

"I knew Brad didn't want children, but I brushed that aside. I was so sure he would change his mind as time went by. We worked very, very hard and we did really well together. The business was a huge success. Then I got pregnant."

She saw the question in his eyes and she shook her head. "No, it was purely and simply an accident."

She bit her lip and looked toward the window for a moment, steadying her voice.

"But I never dreamed Brad would reject it so totally. He just wouldn't accept it." She looked back into his eyes, searching for understanding. "I thought we could work things out. After all, we loved each other. These things happen in life. You deal with them. You make adjustments. You move on."

"Not Brad," he guessed.

"No. Not Brad." She shrugged. "He said, get rid of them."

He drew in a sharp breath. It was almost a gasp. She could hear it in the silence of the kitchen, and she winced.

"And you said?"

She shrugged again. "I'd rather die."

Connor nodded. He knew her well enough

to know that was the truth. What the hell was Brad thinking?

"Suddenly he was like a stranger to me. He just shut the door. He went down to Portland to open up a branch office for our business. I thought he would think it over and come back and…" She gave him a significant look. "But he never came back. He began to make the branch office his headquarters. Then you showed up and told me he wanted a divorce."

Connor nodded. His voice was low and gruff as he asked her, "Do you want him back?"

She had to think about that one. If she was honest, she would have to admit there was a part of her—a part she wasn't very proud of— that would do almost anything to get him back. Anything but the one thing he asked for.

She stared at him and wondered how much she should tell him. He was obviously surprised to know about how little Brad cared about his sons. A normal man would care. So Brad had turned out to be not very normal. That was her mistake. She should have realized that and never married him in the first place.

She also had to live with the fact that he was getting worse and worse about paying child support. There were so many promises—and then so many excuses. What there wasn't a lot of was money.

The business was floundering, he said. He was trying as hard as he could, but the profits weren't rolling in like they used to in the old days—when she was doing half the work. Of course, he didn't mention that. He didn't want her anywhere near the business anymore.

She knew he resented having to give her anything. After all, he'd given her the house—not that it was paid off. Still, it had been what she wanted, what she felt she had to have to keep a stable environment for the boys.

But now she was having a hard time making the mortgage payments. She had to make a go of her cake business, or else she would have to go back to work and leave the boys with a baby-sitter. She was running out of time.

Time to build her business up to where it could pay for itself. Time to stabilize the mortgage situation before the bank came down on her. Time to get the boys old enough so that when she did have to go for a real, paying job, it wouldn't break her heart to leave them with strangers.

So, yes. What Brad wanted now mattered. Had he gone through a transformation? Had he come up with second thoughts and decided to become a friend to the family? Or was it all more excuses about what he couldn't do instead of what he could? Women with husbands in a stable situation didn't realize how lucky they were.

Funny. Sometimes it almost seemed as though Brad had screwed up her marriage and now he wanted to screw up her single life as well.

She shook her head slowly. "I want my life back," she admitted. "I want the life I had when

I had a loving husband. I want my babies to have their father. But I don't see how that can ever happen."

Her eyes stung and she blinked quickly to make sure no tears dared show up.

"Unless…" She looked up into Connor's eyes. "Unless you have a message from Brad that he wants it to happen, too."

Whistling in the wind. She knew how useless that was. She gave Connor a shaky smile, basically absolving him of all guilt in the matter. She saw the look in his eyes. He felt sorry for her. She cringed inside. She didn't want pity.

"Don't worry. I don't expect that. But I do want to know what he sent you for."

Connor shook his head. Obviously he had nothing to give her. So Brad must have sent him on a scouting expedition, right? To see if she was surviving. To see if she was ready to hoist the white flag and admit he was right and she was wrong. She couldn't make it on her own after all. She should have listened to him. And now, she should knuckle under and take his advice and give it all up.

She bit her lip. She wasn't disappointed, exactly. She knew the score. But she was bummed out and it didn't help her outlook on the day.

A timer went off and she hopped up to check on her cakes. This was where she belonged, this was where she knew what she was doing. The realm of human emotions was too treacherous. She would take her chances with the baked goods.

Connor watched her getting busy again and he wished he could find some way to help her deal with the truth—that Brad didn't want her. He couldn't say it might never happen. Brad could change his mind. But right now, he didn't want Jill at all. What he wanted was to be totally free of her. At least, that was how he'd presented things a few days ago when they'd talked.

Brad wanted that, and he wanted her to give up her remaining interest in the company. That was the message he was supposed to make her listen to. That was the message he just couldn't bring himself to tell her. Maybe later.

He took his cup to the sink, rinsed it out and headed back into the living room. He was folding up the covers he'd used when the front door opened and a young woman hurried in.

Connor looked up and started to smile. It was Sara Darling, Jill's sister, and she stopped dead when she saw who had been sleeping on her sister's couch.

"You!" she said accusingly, and he found himself backing up, just from the fire in her eyes.

He knew that Sara and Jill were very close, but he also knew they tended to see things very differently. Both were beautiful. Where Jill had a head full of crazy curls that made you want to kiss her a lot, Sara wore her blond hair slicked back and sleek, making her look efficient and professional. Today she wore a slim tan linen suit with a pale peach blouse and nude heels and she looked as though she was about to gavel an important business meeting to order.

"What are you doing here?" she demanded of him. "Oh, brother. I should have known you'd show up. Let a woman be vulnerable and alone and it's like sharks smelling blood in the water."

"Hey," he protested, surprised. He'd always been friendly with this woman in the past. "That's a bit harsh."

"Harsh? You want to see harsh?"

He blanched. "Not really."

Okay, so Sara was being extra protective of her sister. He got it. But she'd never looked on him as a bad guy before. Why now? He tried a tentative smile.

"Hey, Sara. Nice to see you."

She was still frowning fiercely. "You have no right to complicate Jill's life."

He frowned, too, but in a more puzzled way. That was actually not what he wanted to do, either. But it seemed he was right. Sara was circling the wagons around her sister. How to convince her she didn't need to do that with him?

"Listen, staying for the night wasn't how I planned this."

"I'll bet." She had her arms crossed and looked very intimidating. "Just what *did* you have in mind, Casanova?"

What? Did she really think he was hovering around in order to catch Jill in an emotional state? If only! He wanted to laugh at her but he knew that would only infuriate her further.

"Listen, I saved your sister from a blind date gone horribly wrong. Seriously. Do you know the guy she went out with?"

Sara shook her head, looking doubtful.

"I think his name was Karl."

She shook her head again.

"Well, if you knew him, you'd see why Jill needed rescuing. He was flamboyantly wrong for her."

"Okay." Sara looked a little less intimidating. "Good. I'm glad you were there to help her out."

He breathed a sigh of relief. She was approachable after all.

"So I brought her back here, planning to drop her off and come back to see her in the morning, but there was a riot going on in the house. The twins had taken the babysitter hostage. I had to stay and help Jill regain the high ground. There was no choice."

It was as though she hadn't heard a word he'd said. She paced slowly back and forth in front of him, glaring like a tiger. It was evident she thought he was exaggerating and she'd already gone back to the root of the problem.

"So…what's the deal?" she said, challenging him with her look. "Brad sent you, didn't he?"

Uh-oh. He didn't want to go there if he could help it. He gave her a fed-up look. "Why does everyone assume I can't make a move on my own?"

She glared all the harder. "If he's trying to get her to come back to him, you can tell him…"

He held up a hand to stop her. It was time to

nip this supposition in the bud. "Sara, no. Brad is not trying to get her back."

"Oh." Her look was pure sarcasm. "So the new honey is still hanging around?"

He ran his fingers through his thick, curly hair and grimaced. "Actually I think that was two or three honeys ago," he muttered, mostly to himself. "But take my word for it, Brad isn't looking for forgiveness. Not yet, anyway."

Her dark eyes flared with outrage, but she kept her anger at a slow simmer. "That's our Brad. Trust him to make life and everything in it all about him and no one else."

He nodded. That was one point they could agree on. "Brad does like to have things go his way."

Sara's gaze had fallen on the plastic bag of items picked up in the yard. She scowled, touching it with the toe of her shoe.

"What's all this?"

"Oh. Uh. I left it there. I'll get it...."

She looked up in horror. "What are you doing, moving in?"

Now he couldn't help it. He had to laugh. "Sara, you don't need to hate me. I'm not the enemy."

"Really? What are you, then?"

"A friend." He tried to look earnest. He'd always thought Sara liked him well enough. He certainly hadn't expected to be attacked with guns blazing this way. "I'm Jill's friend. And I really want what's best for her."

"Sorry, Connor. You can't be a true friend to Jill while you're still any sort of friend to Brad. It won't work."

His head went back and he winced. "That's a little rigid, don't you think?"

She moved closer, glancing toward the kitchen to make sure they weren't being overheard. "If you'd seen what she's gone through over this last year or so, you might change your tune."

"What?" He caught her by the upper arm. "What happened?"

She shook her head, looking away.

"Has Brad been here to see her?"

She looked up at him. "Not that I know of. But he manages to make life miserable for her by long distance."

He frowned, wishing she would be more specific.

She looked at him, shook her head and her shoulders drooped. All her animosity had drained away and tears rimmed her eyes. "Oh, Connor, she deserves so much better. If you could see how hard she works... And every time she turns around, there's some new obstacle thrown in her path. I just can't stand it anymore. It's not fair."

She pulled away and he let her go. And now he was the one whose emotions were roiling. Damn Brad, anyway. Why couldn't he just leave her alone?

He ran his hand through his hair again, tempted to rip chunks of it out in frustration. He had to get out of here. If he wasn't careful, he would get caught up in the need to protect Jill. From what? He wasn't even sure. Life, probably. Just life. As Sara had said, it wasn't fair. But it also wasn't his fight. No, he had to go.

He would drive back to his hotel, check out and head for Portland. He would tell Brad he couldn't help him and advise him to leave Jill alone. Maybe he would even tell his old friend what he really thought of him. It was way past time to do that.

Jill was in a hurry and things weren't working out. She had Tanner dressed in his little play suit, but she couldn't catch Timmy, and now he was streaking around the room, just out of her reach, laughing uproariously.

"Timmy!" she ordered. "You stop right there."

Fat chance of that. He rolled under the bed and giggled as she reached under, trying to grab him.

"You come out of there, you rascal."

She made a lucky grab and caught his foot and

pulled him out, disarming grin and all. "Oh, you little munchkin," she cried, but she pulled him into her arms and held him tightly. Her boys were so precious to her. She'd given up a lot to make sure she would have them. Tears stung her eyelids and she fought them back. She couldn't let herself cry. Not now. She had a day to get through.

She had a huge, wonderful day full of work ahead. A day like this could turn things around, if it started a trend. She heard Sara's voice downstairs and she smiled. What a relief. Good. Sara was here. She would be able to help with the children.

She so appreciated Sara giving her some time like this. She knew she was applying for a promotion. She'd been a contributing editor to the design section of *Winter Bay Magazine* for almost two years and she'd done some fabulous work. If she got the new job, she would be working more hours during the week and wouldn't be able to help out as much. Still, she hoped she got it. She certainly deserved the recognition.

She was thankful for small blessings. Right now, if she had Sara here to help with the twins, and then Trini coming in a half hour to help with the baking and delivery, she would be okay. She would just barely be able to fulfill all the commitments she'd made for the day.

It was a challenge, but she could do it. In fact, she had to do it.

Sara appeared at the doorway just as she finished dressing her boys and sent them into the playroom.

"Hey there," she said, ready to greet her sister with a smile until she saw the look on her face. "What's the matter? What's wrong?"

Sara sighed and shook her head.

"Did you see Connor?" Jill asked brightly. "He looks so much the same, you'd never know he'd been gone for a year and a half, would you?"

Sara gave her a look. "Jill, we've got to talk."

Jill groaned and grabbed her sister's hand. "Not now, sweetie. Not today. I've got so much I've got to get to and…"

Sara was shaking her head. "You've got to get rid of him, Jill."

She frowned. "Who?"

Sara pointed back down the stairs as though he were following her. "Connor. You've got to make him go right away."

Dropping her hand, Jill turned away, feeling rebellious. She'd been thinking the same thing but she didn't want to hear it from anyone else. Connor was hers. She resented anyone else— even her beloved sister—critiquing their relationship. She would make him go when she was good and ready to make him go.

Sara grabbed her by the shoulders. "You know he's just here spying for Brad," she said in a low, urgent voice. "You don't want that, do you?"

Sara had never warmed to Jill's ex-husband, even during the good times. And once he'd gone off and left her high and dry, she'd developed what could only be described as a dogged contempt for the man.

Jill took a deep breath and decided to ignore everything she'd said. Life would be simpler that way.

"What are you doing here so early?" she asked instead, trying to sound bright and cheery. "I appreciate it, but…"

"Oh." Sara's demeanor changed in an instant and she dropped her hold on her sister's shoulders. "Oh, Jill, I came early to tell you…I'm so sorry, but I won't be able to help you today. They want me to fly down to L.A. There's just no way I can get out of it. I'll be meeting with the editorial staff from Chicago and…"

"Today?" Jill couldn't stop the anguish from bursting out as she realized what this meant.

Sara looked stricken. "It's a really bad day, right?"

"Well, I told you I've got a huge stack of orders and…" Jill stopped herself, set her shoulders and got hold of her fears. "No, no." She shook her head. "No, Sara. It's much more important for you to go do this, I'm sure."

Sara grabbed her hand again. "Oh, honey, I'm so sorry, but I really can't turn them down. They want to see how I handle myself with the visiting members." She bit her lip and looked as though she was about to cry. A range of conflicting emotions flashed through her wide dark eyes and then she shook her head decisively. "Oh, forget it. I'll tell them something has come up and I just can't do it. Don't worry. They'll understand. I think."

Jill dismissed all that out of hand. "Don't be ridiculous. Of course you have to go. This is your career. This is something you've worked so hard for."

"But I can't leave you if you really need me."

"But I don't." Jill dug deep and managed a bright smile. "Not really. Trini will be here soon and we'll be able to handle it."

Sara looked worried. "Are you sure?"

"Positive." She smiled again.

"Because I can stay if you really need me. I can tell them…"

"No." She hugged her sister. "You go. You have to go. I will lose all respect for you if you let silly sentiment keep you from achieving your highest goals. Say no more about it. You're gone. It's decided."

"But…"

"Come on. Do it for me. Do it for all of us. Make us proud."

Her smile was almost painful by now, but doggone it—she wasn't going to stop. Sara had to go. No two ways about it. And she would just have to cope on her own. Thank God for Trini.

"So she's really going?" Connor had watched Sara rushing off and then turned to see Jill come down from upstairs with a tense look on her face.

"Yes. Yes, she is."

He noted that her hands were gripped together as though she could hardly stand it. He frowned.

"Do you think you can do it without her?"

She took a deep breath. "It won't be easy. But once Trini gets here, we'll put our noses to the grindstone and work our little tushes off for the next twelve hours. Then you'll see."

He was bemused by her intensity. "What will I see?"

She looked up at him wide-eyed. "That this is serious. Not just a hobby job. It's real."

He frowned. He wanted to tell her that he respected her immensely and that he was impressed with what she was attempting to do here, but before he could get a word out, she went on, pacing tensely as she talked.

"You know, I thought I had everything pretty much under control. My life was running on an even keel. I was beginning to feel as though I might make it after all." She stopped and looked at him with a sense of foreboding wonder. "And then you hit town. And everything went to hell."

She was trying to make it sound like a joke,

but there was too much stress in her voice to carry it off. He winced.

"So you blame me now?"

"Why not? There's nobody else within shouting distance. You're going to have to take the fall." She tried to smile but her mouth was wobbly.

He looked at her, saw the anxious look in her eyes and he melted beyond control. "Jill…" He took her hands in his and drew her closer. "Listen, why don't I stay? I could help you with the boys. I could run errands, answer phones."

She was shaking her head but he didn't wait to hear her thoughts.

He pulled her hands up against his chest. "I want to help you. Really. I know you've had a lot of setbacks lately and I want to help smooth over some rough spots if I can. Come on, Jill. Let me stay."

Her lower lip was trembling as she looked into his eyes. He groaned and pulled her into his arms, holding her tightly against his body. She felt like heaven and he wanted the moment to go on forever, but she didn't let it happen. She was already pulling out of his embrace, and he could have kicked himself for doing it.

Too blatant, Connor old chap, he told himself ruefully. *You really tipped your hand there, didn't you?*

"No, Connor," she said as she pushed him away.

She looked at him, shaken. She'd wanted to melt into his arms. She still felt the temptation so strongly, she had to steel herself against it. She knew it had to be mostly because she was so afraid, so nervous about her ability to meet her challenges. If she let him hold her, she could pretend to forget all that.

And then there was the fact that it had been so long since a man—a real man, a man that she liked—had held her. Karl didn't count. And she hungered for that sort of connection.

But not with Connor. Not with Brad's best friend.

"No. It's sweet of you to offer, but I really can't let you stay. We are going to need to focus like laser beams on this task and having you here won't help." She smiled at him with affection to take the bite out of her words.

He stepped farther from her and avoided her eyes. The sting of her rejection was like a knife to his heart. "Okay then. I guess I'd better get going."

"Yes. I'm sorry."

He started to turn away, then remembered. "Hey, I didn't fix the door I kicked in last night."

She shook her head. "Don't worry. I've already called a handy man I use."

"Oh." He hesitated, but there didn't seem to be much to say. He was superfluous, obviously. Just in the way. Might as well get the hell out.

"Okay. It was good to see you again, Jill."

She smiled at him. "Yes. Come back soon. But next time, don't stop off to see Brad first."

He nodded. "You've got my word on that one,"

he said. He shoved his hands down into the back pockets of his jeans and looked at her, hard.

"What?" she asked, half laughing.

"I just want to get a good picture of you to hold me over," he told her. "Until next time."

The look in her eyes softened and she stepped forward and kissed his cheek. "Goodbye," she whispered.

He wanted to kiss her mouth so badly, he had to clench his teeth together to stop himself from doing it.

"Goodbye," he said softly, then he turned and left the house.

Outside, he felt like hell. He'd had hangovers that hadn't felt this bad. Everything in him wanted to stay and he couldn't do it. He looked down at the ferry dock. There was a ferry there now, loading up. He'd catch it and then it would be all over. How long before he saw her again? Who knew. He would probably go back to Singapore. At least he knew where he stood there.

Swearing softly with a string of obscenities that he rarely used, he slid into the driver's seat and felt for the keys.

"Goodbye to all that," he muttered, then turned on the engine. About to back out, he turned to glance over his shoulder—just in time to see a small economy car come sailing in behind him, jerk to a stop, and block him in.

"Hey," he said.

But the young woman who'd driven up didn't hear him and didn't notice that his engine was running. She flew out of the car and went racing up the walk, flinging herself through the doorway.

Okay. This had to be the famous Trini he'd heard so much about. She'd trapped him in his parking space and he wasn't going to make the ferry. Now what?

CHAPTER FIVE

JILL HADN'T RECOVERED from Connor leaving when Trini came bursting in. The boys ran to her joyfully and she knelt down and collected them into her arms, then looked up. Jill knew immediately that something was wrong.

"Trini, what is it?" she cried.

Trini was young and pretty with a long, swinging ponytail and a wide-eyed expression of constant amazement, as though life had just really surprised her once again. And in this case, it seemed to be true.

"You'll never guess!" she cried, and then she burst into tears. "Oh, Jill," she wailed, "this is so good and so bad at the same time."

"What is it, sweetheart?" Jill asked, pulling her up and searching her face. But she thought she knew. And she dreaded what she was about to hear.

"Oh, Jill, I just got the call and..." She sobbed for a moment, then tried again. "I got in. I was on the wait list and they just called. I got accepted into the program at Chanoise Culinary Institute in New York."

"But...hasn't the quarter already started?"

"Yes, but they had two people drop out already. So they called and said if I could get there by tomorrow, I'm in."

"Trini! That's wonderful! You deserve a space in the class. I always knew that."

But did it have to be today? She couldn't help but wish the timing had been different. Still, this was wonderful for Trini.

"What can I do to help you?"

Trini shook her head. "You've already done enough. You wrote the recommendation that got me in." She sighed happily, and then she frowned with worry. "The only bad part is I have to leave right away. My flight leaves at noon. The Jamison engagement party..."

"Don't you think twice, Trini. You just get out of here and go pack and prepare for the best experience of your life. Okay?"

Trini threw her arms around Jill's neck and Jill hugged her tightly. "I'm so excited," Trini cried. "Oh, Jill, I'll keep you posted on everything we do. And when I come back..."

"You'll teach me a thing or two, I'm sure." She smiled at her assistant, forcing back any hint of the panic she was feeling. "Now off with you. You need to get ready for the rest of your life."

"I will. Wish me luck!"

"I'll definitely wish you luck. You just supply the hard work!"

Trini laughed and dashed out the door. Jill reached out to put her hand on the back of a chair to keep herself from collapsing. She could hardly breathe. She saw Connor standing in the entryway. She didn't know why he'd come back and right now, she couldn't really think about it or talk to him. She was in full-scale devastation meltdown mode.

What was she going to do? What on earth was she going to do? She couldn't think a coherent thought. Her mind was a jumble. She knew she was standing on the edge of the cliff and if she lost her balance, she was going over. She couldn't let that happen. She had to get herself together.

But what was the use? She'd fought back so often. So much kept going wrong and she kept trying to fix things. They just wouldn't stay fixed. She was so tired. Today, right now, she wanted to quit. There had to be a way to give up, to surrender to reality. She just couldn't do this anymore.

Looking at her reflection in the hall mirror, she muttered sadly, "Okay. I get it. I'm not meant to do this. I should quit banging my head against the wall. I should quit, period. Isn't that what a sane, rational person would do?"

She stared at herself, feeling cold and hollow. She knew Connor was still watching her, that he'd heard what she said, but she hardly cared. She was in such deep trouble, what did it matter if he saw her anguish? But a part of her was grateful for his presence—and that he was keeping back, not trying to comfort her right now. She didn't need that since there was no comfort, was no real hope.

She stared at herself for a long moment, teetering between the devil and the deep blue sea. That was how it felt. No matter what she did, disaster seemed inevitable.

Then, gradually, from somewhere deep inside, she began to put her strength back together and pull her nerve back into place. She took a giant breath and slowly let it out. She wouldn't surrender. She would go down fighting, no matter what it cost her. Let them try to stop her! She had glaze to prepare. She had cakes to bake. She would try her best to get this done and on time. She could only do what she could do— but she would do the best she could.

She looked at herself in the mirror again and gave herself a small, encouraging smile. She needed a joke right now, something to help her put things into perspective. She was a baking woman—hear her roar! They would have to pry her baking mitts off her cold, dead hands.

Revived and reinvigorated, she turned to face Connor. "There," she said. "I'm better now."

He still appeared a bit worried, but he'd watched her mini-breakdown and the instant rebuild in awe.

"Wow," he said. "Jill, you are something else."

She sighed. "You weren't supposed to see that."

"I'm glad I did. I've got more faith in you than ever."

She laughed. "I've got to get back to work." She frowned. "Why are you still here?"

"Because I'm not going to go while you still need me."

"What makes you think I need you?" Turning, she headed into the kitchen.

"So," he said tentatively, following her. "Now your number one assistant has bailed on you. And your sister has bailed on you." He shrugged. "Who you gonna call? You need someone else. Who can come to your rescue?"

She met his gaze. "There's nobody. Really. I've tried to find backup before. There's really nobody. This island is too small. There aren't enough people to draw on."

He nodded. "That's what I thought." He picked up an apron someone had thrown on the chair and began to tie it on himself. "Okay. Tell me what to do."

Her eyes widened. "What are you talking about?"

His face was so earnest, she felt her breath catch in her throat. He really meant it.

"How can I help you, Jill? What can I do?"

This was so sweet of him, but it couldn't work. He didn't have the skills, the background. And anyway, he wasn't here for her. He was here for Brad. There was no denying it.

"Just stay out of the way." She shrugged help-lessly. He shouldn't be here at all. Why was he? "Go back to your hotel. You don't belong here."

He shook his head. "No."

"Connor!"

He shook his head again. "You're like a fish flopping around on the pier, gasping for breath. You need help, lady. And I'm going to give it to you."

She shook her own head in disbelief. "You can't cook."

"The hell I can't."

Her gaze narrowed. "I don't believe it."

He stepped closer, towering over her and star-ing down with cool deliberation. "There are a whole lot of things about me you just don't have a clue about, Miss Know-it-all."

She shook her head, still wary. "Look, just because you can fry up a mean omelet after midnight for your Saturday night date doesn't mean you can cook. And it certainly doesn't mean you can bake."

"I'm not proposing to be your baker. You've got that slot nailed. I'm signing on as an assistant. I'm ready to assist you in any way I can."

He meant it. She could see the resolve in his eyes. But how could he possibly be a help rather than a hindrance? There was no way he could get up to speed in time. Still, she was in an awful bind here.

"So you can cook?" she asked him skeptically.

"Yes."

"There's a difference between cooking and baking."

"I know that." He shook his head impatiently. "Jill, you're the baker. But you need a support staff and I'm going to be it."

"But...what are you planning to do?"

"Prep pans, wash pans, drizzle on glaze, pack product for delivery, deliver product, go for supplies, answer the phones..."

She was beginning to smile. Maybe she was being foolish, but she didn't have much choice, did she? "And the most important thing?" she coached.

He thought for a moment, then realized what she was talking about.

"Keep an eye on the boys," he said and was rewarded with a quick smile. "You got it. In fact, I'll do anything and everything in order to leave you room to practice your creative artistry."

"My what?" She laughed and gave him a push. "Oh, Connor, you smooth talker you."

"That's what it is." He took her by the shoulders and held her as though she was very, very special. "I've eaten some of your cake wizardry, lady. *Magnifique!*"

The word hung in the air. She gazed up at him, suddenly filled with a wave of affection. Had she ever noticed before how his eyes crinkled in the corners? And how long his beautiful dark lashes were? Reaching out, she pressed her palm to his cheek for just a moment, then drew it back and turned away so that he wouldn't see the tears beginning to well in her eyes.

"Okay," she said a little gruffly. "We'll give it a try. As long as you turn out to be worth more than the trouble you cause." But she glanced back with a smile, showing him that she was only teasing.

"I won't get in your way, I swear. You just wait and see. We'll work together like a well-oiled machine."

She blinked back the tears and smiled at him. "You promise?"

"Cross my heart and hope to die."

"Ooh, don't say that. Bad vibes." She shook her head. "Okay then. Here's the game plan. I'm going to go back over all my recipes and check to make sure I've got the right supplies before I start mixing new batters. You go and see what the boys are up to. Then you come back and help me."

He saluted her like a soldier. *"Mais oui, mon chef."*

"Wow. Those sleepy-time French lessons really did do some good. And here I was a non-believer."

He looked a bit nonplussed himself. "Every now and then a few French words just seem to burst out of me, so yeah, I guess so."

He turned his attention to the twins not a moment too soon. There was a ruckus going on in the next room. The boys were crying. Someone had pushed someone down and grabbed away his toy. The other one was fighting to get it back. Happened all the time. They needed supervision.

But there was really no time today to deal with it properly. He went back to discuss the situation with Jill.

"If you can think of any strenuous activities, something that might make them take their naps a bit earlier..." she mused, checking the supply of flavorings and crossing them off a list, then handing the list to him to start working on an inventory of the flour she had in storage.

"Say no more," He gave her a wise look. "I've got a trick or two up my sleeve. As soon as I finish counting up the canisters, I'll deal with those little rascals."

Time was racing by. Her convection oven could accommodate four cakes at a time, but they had to be carefully watched.

"We've got to get these done by noon," she told him. "I can't start the mini Bundts any later than that. We've got to get the minis done by three, glazed and packed by four-thirty, and off for delivery by five."

He nodded. He knew she wasn't completely resigned to him being there with her. This was her biggest day and her eyes betrayed how worried she was. Her shoulders looked tight. She wasn't confident that they could do it, even working hard together.

He only hoped he could—what? Help her? That went without saying. Protect her? Sure. That was his main goal. Always had been. If only he'd realized earlier that his vague distrust of Brad was based on more than jealousy. It seemed to be real in ways that were only now becoming more and more clear to him. It was a good thing she'd reconciled herself to accepting his help, because he knew he couldn't go. He couldn't leave her on her own. He had to be here for her.

Meanwhile, he had to find a way to wear out the boys. He tried to recall his own childhood, but eighteen months old was a little too far back to remember much. Still, he had a few ideas.

He took the boys out into the backyard. There was a big sloping hill covered with grass. Improvising, he set up a racetrack with different stations where the boys had to perform simple modified gymnastic elements in order to move on to the next station.

They loved it. They each had a natural competitive spirit that came out in spades as they began to understand the goals involved. Each wanted to win with a naive gusto that made him laugh out loud. They were a great pair of twins.

They were so into it. Running up the hill took a lot of their time. Shrieking with excitement was a factor. And Connor found he was having as much fun as they were.

At one point, he had them racing uphill, each pulling a red wagon filled with rocks to see who could get to the top first. He'd brought along lots of prizes, including pieces of hard candy that they loved. He knew they were sure to rot teeth, but he would only use them today and never again. Or not often, anyway. He also made sure to keep the winnings pretty equal between the two of them, so that each could shine in turn.

But, as he told Jill a bit later, the one drawback was—no matter how tired he made them, he was even more so. He was pitifully out of shape.

But it was fun. That was the surprising part. The boys were a couple of great kids, both so eager, so smart. He wondered what Brad would think if he could see them. How could he possibly resist these two?

He brought them back in and settled them down to watch an educational DVD while he went down to the kitchen to see what he could do to help Jill. She had recently pulled four cakes out of the oven and she was ready to put on a glaze.

"Show me how," he told her. "You're going to need help when you glaze all those small cakes for the engagement party, aren't you?"

She looked at him with some hesitation, and he saw it right away. Reaching out, he took her hands in his.

"Jill, I'm not here to take over," he said. "I don't expect to start making decisions or judging you. I'm here to do anything you tell me to do. You talk. I'll listen."

She nodded, feeling a little chagrined. She knew he meant well. He was just here to help her. Why couldn't she calm her fears and let him do just that?

As she glanced up, her gaze met his and she had an impulse that horrified her. She wanted to throw herself into his arms, close her eyes and hold on tightly.

The same thing she'd felt before when he'd held her came back in a wave and she felt dizzy with it. She wanted his warmth and his comfort, wanted it with a fierce craving that ached inside her. She couldn't give in to that feeling. Turning away quickly, she hoped he couldn't see it in her eyes.

She was just feeling weak and scared. That was what it had to be. She couldn't let herself fall into that trap.

"Okay. I'm going to teach you everything I know about putting on a glaze," she said resolutely. "And believe me, it's simple. We'll start with a basic sugar glaze. You'll pick it up in no time at all."

He learned fast and she went ahead and taught him how to make a caramel glaze as well, including tricks on how not to let the sugar burn and how to roast the chopped pecans before you added them to make them crisper and more flavorful. She then showed him how to center the cakes on the lacy doilies she used in the fancy boxes she packed the cakes in before transporting them.

"Each cake should look like it's a work of art on its own," she told him. "Never ever let a cake look like you just shoved it into a box to get it where it needs to go. They should look like they're being carried in a golden coach, on their way to the ball."

He grinned. "Cinderella cakes?"

"Exactly. They have to look special. Otherwise, why not pick up a cake at the grocery store?"

That was when his phone rang. It made him jerk. He knew before he even looked at the screen who it was. Brad. Brad wondering how things were going. Brad, wondering if he'd talked her into committing to his plan. Brad, trying to control everything, just like always.

He put the phone on vibrate and shoved it into his pocket.

Once they'd finished the glazing, he went back to babysitting, making peanut butter and jelly sandwiches for the boys. They looked so good, he made one for himself. Then he raided the refrigerator and made a cool, crisp salad for Jill.

"Lunchtime," he told her, once he'd set the boys down to eat at their little table in their playroom.

She gave one last look at her boxed creations, snuck a peek at the new cakes in the oven and turned to him with a smile.

"So far, so good," she said as she sat down across from him at the kitchen table. "Though one disaster can throw the whole schedule off."

"Relax," he said. "No disaster would dare ruin this day for you."

"Knock on wood," she said, doing just that. She took a bite of salad and made a noise of pleasure. "Ah! This is so refreshing." She cocked her head to the side. "The boys are being awfully good."

He nodded. "So it seems. I gave them their sandwiches."

She frowned. "You left them alone with food?"

"They seemed to be doing great when I looked in on them." He glanced toward the doorway. "Though they sure seem quiet."

Jill's eyes widened. "Too quiet," she cried, vaulting out of her chair and racing for the playroom. Visions of peanut butter masterpieces smeared on walls and teddy bears covered in sticky jam shot through her head.

Connor came right behind her. He didn't have as much experience with what might go wrong, but he could imagine a few things himself.

They skidded around the corner and into the room, only to find a scene of idyllic contentment. The peanut butter sandwiches were half eaten and lay on the table. The boys were completely out, both lying in haphazard fashion wherever they were when sleep snuck up on them. Jill turned and grinned at him.

"You did wear them out. Wow."

They lifted them carefully and put them down in the travel cribs that sat waiting against the far wall. Jill pulled light covers over each of them and they tiptoed out of the room and back to the kitchen.

"They look like they'll sleep for hours," she said hopefully.

"Maybe days," he added to the optimism, but she laughed.

"Doubtful. Besides, we'll miss them if they stay away that long."

"Will we?" he questioned, but he was smiling. He believed her.

She glanced at her watch. "We've got time for a nice long lunch," she said. "Maybe fifteen whole minutes. Those cakes have to be delivered by noon, but the church hall where they're going is only two blocks away. So let's sit down and enjoy a break."

She watched as he settled in across from her and began to eat his sandwich. She was so glad he'd talked her into letting him stay to help. Without him, she would surely be chasing her children up and down the stairs by now, with cakes burning in the background. She raised her glass of iced tea at him.

"To Connor McNair, life saver," she said. "Hip, hip, hooray."

He laughed. "Your Bundt cakes aren't all out of the fire yet," he told her with a crooked grin. "Don't count your chickens too soon."

"Of course not. I just wanted to acknowledge true friendship when it raises its furry head."

He shook his head and had to admit it was almost as covered with curls as hers. "Anytime," he told her, then tried to warble it as a tune. "Anytime you need me, I'll be there."

Her gaze caught his and she smiled and whispered, "Don't get cocky, kid."

His gaze deepened. "Why not?" he whispered

back. "What's the fun of life if you don't take chances?"

She held her breath. For just a few seconds, something electric seemed to spark between them. And then it was gone, but she was breathing quickly.

"Chances. Is that what you call it?" she said, blinking a bit.

He nodded. "Chances between friends. That's all."

She frowned at him. "Some friend. Where were you to stop me from marrying Brad?"

The look in his face almost scared her. She'd meant it in a lighthearted way, but being casual about a subject that cut so deep into her soul didn't really work. Emotions were triggered. Her joke had fallen flat.

"I tried," he said gruffly, a storm brewing in his blue eyes.

He was kidding—wasn't he?

"What do you mean?" she asked, trying to ignore the trembling she heard in her own voice.

He leaned back in his chair but his gaze never left hers. "Remember? The night before your wedding."

She thought back. "Yes. Wait. You didn't even go to the bachelor party."

He snorted. "I went. Hell, I was hosting it." He seemed uncomfortable. "But I couldn't stay. I couldn't take all the celebration."

"Oh."

"So I went off and left all those happy guys to their revelry. I got a bottle of Scotch and took it to a sandy beach I knew of."

She nodded slowly, thinking back. "As I remember it, you were pretty tanked when you showed up at my apartment."

He took a deep breath and let it out. "Yes. Yes, I was. I was a tortured soul."

"Really? What were you so upset about that night?"

He stared at her. Couldn't she guess? Was she really so blind? He'd been out of his head with agony that night. He knew what a wonderful girl Jill was, knew it and loved her for it. And he knew Brad wasn't going to make her happy. But how could he tell her that? How could he betray a friend?

The problem was, he had to betray one of them. They were both his best friends and he couldn't stand to see them getting married. And at the same time, he didn't think he should interfere. It was their decision. Their misfortune. Their crazy insane absolutely senseless leap into the brave unknown.

But he knew a thing or two, didn't he? He knew some things he was pretty sure she didn't know. But how could he hurt her with them? How could he explain to her about all the times Brad had cheated on her in the years they'd all been friends?

She would chalk it up to pure jealousy, and in a way, she would have been right. He was jealous. He wanted her. He knew Brad didn't value her enough. He knew Brad didn't deserve her. But how could he tell her that? How could he tell her the truth without ending up with her despising him more than she now did Brad? If she really did.

Besides, what could he offer her in place of her romance with Brad? He wasn't even sure he would ever be ready for any sort of full-time, long-term relationship. Every now and then he thought he'd conquered his background and the wariness he felt. But then he would see examples among his friends that just brought it back again. Could you trust another human in the long run? Was it worth the effort, just to be betrayed in the end?

And so—the Scotch. The alcohol was supposed to give him the courage to do what had to be done. But it didn't work that way. It made him sick instead, and he babbled incoherently once he had Jill's attention. She never understood what he was trying to say.

He couldn't even tell her now. She'd asked him a direct question. What was he so upset about that night? And still, he couldn't tell her the truth.

Because I knew you were marrying the wrong man. You should have been marrying me.

Reaching out, he caught her hand and looked deep into her eyes.

"Jill, tell me what you want. What you need in your life to be happy."

She stared back at him, and he waited, heart beating a fast tattoo on his soul.

"Connor," she began, "I… I don't know how to explain it exactly, but I…"

But then she shook her head and the timer went off and they both rose to check the cakes. Whatever she'd been about to say was lost in a cloud of the aroma of delicious confections.

The last full-size cakes came out and were set to cool and they began to fill the large mini Bundt cake pans. Twelve little cakes per pan. And each had to be filled to exactly the same level.

"They'll take about fifteen to twenty minutes," she told him nervously. "Then the ovens have to be back up to temperature before we put the next batch in. If we time it right, we might just make it. But it's going to be close."

One hundred and ten little cakes, she thought with a tiny surge of hysteria. Oh, my!

Connor left to deliver some of the full-size cakes. Jill checked on the babies. They were still sleeping in their travel cribs. She was thankful for that. Back to the kitchen, she began to prepare the rectangular boxes with the small dividers she was going to put the mini cakes in once they were ready to go. Then Connor was back and they pulled a batch out.

"These are perfect," she said with a sigh of relief. "You get the next batch ready. I'll make the Limoncello glaze."

They both had their eyes on the clock. Time seemed to go so quickly. Minutes seemed to evaporate into thin air. Jill was moving as fast as she could.

And then the phone started ringing. People

who hadn't had their deliveries yet were wondering why.

"We're working as fast as we can," she told them. "Please, every minute I spend on the phone means your cake will get there that much later."

It was starting to feel hopeless. A batch overflowed its pan and they had to pull it out, clean up the mess and start again. She mixed up three batches of glaze and accidentally knocked them over onto the floor. That had to be done again.

And the clock was ticking.

She felt as though the beating of her heart was a clock, racing her, mocking her, letting her know she wasn't going to make it. Biting her lip, she forced back that feeling and dug in even harder.

"Last batch going in," Connor called.

She hurried over to see if it was okay. It was fine. Connor was turning out to be a godsend.

It was almost time. The phone rang. It was the Garden Club wondering where their cake was.

"Their party isn't until seven tonight," she said in full annoyance mode. "Can't they wait?"

"I'll run it over," Connor offered.

"You will not," she told him. "The engagement party is next. We have to deliver to them by five or we will have failed."

The twins woke up and were cranky. Connor tried to entertain them but there was very little hope. They wanted their mother.

Jill had to leave Connor alone with the cakes while she cuddled her boys and coaxed them into a better mood. She knew they needed her and she loved them to pieces, but all the while she felt time passing, ticking, making her crazy. She had to get back to the cakes.

Connor had his own problems. His phone was vibrating every fifteen minutes. Every call was from Brad. He knew that without even checking. He had no intention of answering the phone, but every time it began to move, he had that sinking feeling again.

Brad. Why couldn't he just disappear?

Instead he was texting. Connor didn't read the texts. There was no point to it. He knew what they said.

Brad wanted answers. He wanted to know what was going on. He wanted to get the latest scoop on Jill. All things Connor had no intention of giving him. But knowing Brad, that wasn't going to satisfy him. He was going to intrude, one way or another. And he wouldn't wait long to make his influence felt. Connor looked at his phone. If only there was some way to cut the link to Brad and his expectations.

CHAPTER SIX

IT WAS TIME. They had to move. But the twins wouldn't stop clinging to Jill.

Connor had an idea. He brought in a huge plastic tub he found in the garage, placing it in an empty corner of the kitchen, far from the oven and the electric appliances. Using a large pitcher, he put a few inches of barely warm water in the bottom.

"Hey kids," he called to them. "Want to go swimming?"

He didn't have to offer twice. They were excited, getting into their swimsuits and finding swim toys. Jill could get back to packing up her cakes and Connor could supervise the play area while he worked on glazing at the same time.

The long, rectangular boxes were filled with cakes for the Jamison engagement party. It was time to go. Connor packed them into Jill's van and took off. Jill sat down beside the tub of water to watch her boys pretend to swim and she felt tears well up in her eyes. They had made it. Now—as long as they didn't poison everyone at the engagement party, things would calm down. There were still a few cakes to deliver, but nothing was the hectic job the engagement party had been. She'd come through. And she couldn't have done it without Connor.

She wrapped her arms around her knees and hugged tightly. "Thank you, Connor," she whispered to the kitchen air. "You saved my life. I think I love you."

And she did. Didn't she? She always had. Not the way she loved Brad. But Brad was always such a problem and Connor never was.

She remembered when Brad had been the coolest guy around. The guy everyone looked up to, the hunk every girl wanted to be with. He drove the coolest convertible, had the best parties, knew all the right people. At least, that was the way it seemed back then. And he had chosen her. It was amazing how much you could grow up in just a few years and learn to see beyond the facade.

"Cool" didn't mean much when you had babies to feed in the middle of the night. And it only got in the way when it was time to separate your real friends from the posers. Back then, she'd been a pretty rotten judge of character. She'd improved. She had a better idea of what real worth was.

A half hour later, Connor was back. She rose to meet him, ready to ask him how it went, but he didn't give her time to do that. Instead he came right for her, picked her up and swung her around in a small celebratory dance.

"You did it," he said, smiling down into her face. "The cakes are delivered and the customer is in awe. You met the challenge. Congrats."

"We did it, you mean," she said, laughing as he swung her around again. "Without you, all would be lost right now."

He put her down and shrugged. "What do we still have to get delivered?" he asked. "I want to get this job over with so we can relax." He looked down at the boys, still splashing about in the water. "Hey, guys. How are you doing?"

Timmy laughed and yelled something incomprehensible, and Tanner blew bubbles his way.

"Great," Connor said back, then looked at Jill. "Your orders, *mon chef?*" he asked.

"We do have two deliveries left," she said. "The last cakes are baking right now. We should be ready to call it a day in about an hour. Can you make it until then?"

"Only if I get a fair reward," he said, raising an eyebrow. "What are you offering?"

"I've got nothing," she said, making a face. "Unless you'll take kisses."

She was teasing, just having fun, but it hit him like a blow to the heart. "Kisses are my favorite," he told her gruffly, his eyes darkening.

She saw that, but it didn't stop her. Reaching

up, she planted a kiss on his mouth, then drew back and laughed at him.

He laughed back, but his pulse was racing. "Hey, I'll work for those wages any day," he told her, and then he had to turn away. There was a longing welling up in him. He'd felt it before and he knew what it was.

He'd been yearning for Jill since the day he met her. His own background and emotional hiccups had worked against him letting her know over that first year, and by the time he actually knew what he wanted, Brad had taken over, and it was too late.

"What kind of glaze are we putting on these last cakes?" he asked her.

Jill didn't answer right away. She'd seen the look that had come over his face, noticed his reaction to her friendly kiss. For some reason, her heart was beating in a crazy way she wasn't used to.

"Those get a rum caramel with roasted

chopped pecans sprinkled on top," she said at last.

They worked on it together, but there was a new feeling between them, a sort of sense of connection, that hadn't been there before. And she had to admit, she rather liked it.

He took out the last deliveries and stopped to pick up a pizza on his way home. She had the boys dried and put into their pajamas by then. They got their own special meals and then were put into the playroom to play quietly and get ready for bed. Jill set out the pizza on the kitchen table and she and Connor ate ravenously.

"Wow," he said with a groan. "What a day. I've worked in a lot of places, but I've never been put through the wringer like I was today."

"You did great," she responded. "I couldn't have met the deadlines without you."

He sighed. "What's the outlook for tomorrow?"

Tomorrow? She hadn't allowed herself to

think that far ahead. Was he going to leave tonight? She didn't think so. He didn't seem to be making any of the pertinent preparations. And if he stayed tonight, what about tomorrow? Would he stay then, too? Should she let him?

"Just a couple of orders," she said. "And then, for the rest of the week, not a thing."

"Oh." He looked at her with a guilty grimace. "Uh, maybe you'd better take a look at some of the orders I took over the phone today. I wrote them down somewhere."

That started a mad scramble to locate the paper he'd written them down on.

"I have to set up a system," she muttered once they'd found it. "What if you'd gone and never told me about these?"

Gone? Where was he going?

Their gazes met and the question was there and neither of them wanted to answer it.

She looked at him, at his handsome face, his strong shoulders, and she felt a wave of affection. There was no one else she would have rather spent this day with. It had to be him.

She stopped in front of him and smiled, putting a hand flat on his chest. "Thank you," she said solemnly. "I can never stop thanking you enough. You really did make the difference today."

He didn't smile, but there was a dark, cloudy look in his eyes and he put his own hand over hers. "I wish I could do more," he said, and she could have sworn his voice cracked a little.

She shook her head, wishing she had the right to kiss him the way you would a lover. "You saved me from the nightmares," she murmured.

He frowned. "What nightmares."

She shrugged, wishing she hadn't brought it up. "Sometimes I have this dream where I'm all alone on an island that's being attacked by huge black birds. They look sort of like vultures. They peck away at me. I run and run and they swoop down. Every time I turn to fight one off, others attack from behind me." She shuddered.

His hand tightened over hers. "Bummer."

She tried to smile but her lips were trembling. "No kidding."

"Hey." He leaned forward and dropped a soft kiss on her mouth. "I had a dream about birds last night, too. Only my dream was about a beautiful huge white bird with lacy wings. I was desperately trying to catch her. And you know what? That bird was you."

She smiled, enchanted, and he kissed her again. "Connor," she whispered warningly, trying to draw back, and a shout from one of the boys gave her statement emphasis. He straightened and watched as she left him.

They both went up to put the boys to bed.

"They're just going to climb out of these cribs again," Connor whispered to her.

"Shh. Don't remind them of the possibilities."

They covered the boys and turned out the lights and left, hoping for the best.

"How about a glass of wine?" he asked her.

She hesitated, knowing it would put her right to sleep. "I'd better not," she said. "But you go ahead."

The phone rang. She sighed. She was completely exhausted and ready to go to bed early and try to recoup. Hopefully this wasn't one of her friends asking about the date last night. She'd already ignored a couple of those calls on her cell. And if it was an order for a cake, she only hoped she would be able to get the facts straight.

"Hello?" she said, stifling a yawn. "Jill's Cakes."

"Oh, thank goodness," said the lady on the other end of the line. "You're there. Now please, please don't tell me you're closed for the night."

Jill frowned. What the heck did that mean? Was it someone at the engagement party who thought some of their order was missing? Or something different? "Well, uh, we're here and cleaning up but our workday is pretty much over. Was there something you needed?"

"Oh, Jill, this is Madeline Green," she responded in a voice that could summon cows. "You know me from the church choir."

"Of course." She pulled the phone a bit away from her ear and glanced up at Connor who had come close and was listening. She gave him a shrug. "Nice to hear from you, Madeline."

"Honey, listen. I'm here at the Elks lodge. We've had a disaster. Our caterer has failed us. We have one hundred and two people here for dinner and we have no dessert."

"Oh." No. Her brain was saying, *"No!"* Her body was saying, *"No!"* "I see. Uh….maybe you should go out and buy some ice cream."

"Impossible. We have to have a special dessert. It's traditional. People expect it. This is Old Timers' Night. Some only come to this annual award dinner because of the fancy desserts we usually serve. It's everyone's favorite part."

"But you had some ordered?"

"Oh, yes. They never showed up. The caterer disavows all knowledge of what the pastry chef was up to. He washes his hands of it entirely."

"I see." Her brain was still shrieking, "No!"

"Have you tried the Swedish bakery?"

"They're closed. In fact, everyone is closed. You're our only hope."

Jill blinked. "So you called everyone else first?"

"Well…"

"Never mind." She made a face, but the lady couldn't see it. She took a deep breath. "Madeline, I'm afraid we just can't…"

Suddenly she was aware that Connor had grabbed her upper arm and was shaking her gently.

"Say 'yes,'" he hissed at her intensely.

"What?" she mouthed back, covering the receiver with her hand. "Why?"

"Say 'yes.' Never ever say 'no.'"

He meant it. She groaned.

"You're trying to build up a reputation," he whispered close to her ear. "You need to be the go-to person, the one they can always depend on. If you want to build your business up, you have to go the extra mile."

He was right. She knew he was right. But she was so tired. She really didn't want to do this.

"Say 'yes'," he insisted.

She was too limp to fight it. Uncovering the mouthpiece, she sighed and handed the phone to him. "You do it," she said.

She turned around and looked at the mess they would have to wade through to get this done. Everything in her rebelled.

"You realize how many they need, don't you?" she asked when Connor hung up.

"Yes. We can do it."

"Can we? What makes you think you can say that?"

"I've seen you work. And I'm here to help you."

She winced. "How long do we have?"

"One hour."

Her mouth dropped open but no sound came out.

"Okay," Connor said quickly, hoping to forestall any forecasts of doom. "Think fast. What do you make that cooks in less than an hour?"

She shrugged. She felt like a wrung-out rag. "Cookies."

"Then we make cookies."

She frowned. "But that's not special."

"It is the way we make them." He looked at her expectantly. "What'll we do?"

She looked at him and she had to smile, shaking her head. She knew he was as beat as she was, but the call for desserts seemed to have given him new life. "You're the one who made the promises. You tell me."

"Come on. What's your signature cookie?"

She closed her eyes. "I'm too tired to think."

"Me, too," he agreed stoutly. "So we'll go on instinct instead of brainpower."

She began to laugh. This was all so ridiculous.

They'd just produced more baked product than she'd ever done before in one day, and now they were going to do more? Impossible.

"Cookies?" he coaxed.

"I guess."

They made cookies. Pecan lace cookies with a touch of cardamom, pressed together like sandwiches with mocha butter cream filling between them. Chocolate ganache on the base. A touch of white butter cream around the edges, like a lacy frill.

Connor used the mixer while Jill prepped the pans and got the chocolate ready to melt. Just as the first pan went into the oven, they heard the sound of giggling from the next room.

Jill looked at Connor. "Oh, no."

He nodded. "They climbed out again. We should have known they would." He looked at her. There was no time to spare and she was the chef. "I'll take care of them," he told her. "You just keep baking."

It took a couple of minutes to catch the boys

and carry them back up, and all the while, he was racking his brain to think of some way to keep them in their beds. There was only one idea that just might work, but he knew instinctively that Jill wasn't going to like it. They didn't have much choice. He was going to have to do it and deal with the consequences later.

CHAPTER SEVEN

BY THE TIME Connor got back to the kitchen, Jill had at least sixty cookies cooling and was beginning assembly of the desserts.

"I don't hear the boys," she said. "What did you do?"

"Don't worry. I took care of it."

She stopped and looked at him through narrowed eyes. "You didn't tie them up or anything like that, did you?"

"No, nothing like that. I'd show you, but right now, we've got to hurry with this stuff."

She gave him a penetrating glance, but she was in the middle of the drizzle across the top of each confection and her attention got diverted.

"What do you think?" she asked him.

Connor looked the sample over with a critical eye.

"I don't know. It still needs something. Something to make it look special."

They both stared for a long sixty seconds.

"I know," he said. "We've got plenty of buttercream left. Get your decorating thingamajig."

"Why?"

"I've seen the flowers you can make with butter cream frosting. You're going to make one hundred and two rose buds."

"Oh." She looked at the clock. "Do you really think we can get them out in time?"

"I know we can." He grinned at her, then swooped in and kissed her hard on her pretty mouth. "We can do anything. We already have."

He took her breath away, but she stayed calm. At least outwardly. She stared at him for a few seconds, still feeling that kiss. Why was he doing things guaranteed to send her into a tailspin if she didn't hold herself together?

But she went back to work and she kept control and the job got finished. And at the end, they stared at each other.

"We did it."

"We did, didn't we?"

"But the delivery…"

"Quick. We're five minutes late."

He piled the desserts in boxes and headed for the door. Just before he disappeared, he called back, "Better check on the twins."

She was already on her way. There wasn't a sound as she climbed the stairs. When she opened the door, nothing moved. But somehow everything looked a little wrong. In the dark, she couldn't quite figure out what it was and she hated to turn on the light, but she had to. And what she saw left her speechless.

"What?"

One crib stood empty. The other had been turned upside down. The mattress was on the ground, but the rest of the crib was above it like a cage. And on the mattress, her two little boys were sound asleep.

Her first impulse was to wake them up and rescue them, but then she realized they were probably better off where they were. After all, how was she going to get them to stay in their cribs without the bars?

She went back down, not sure what to do. She started cleaning up the kitchen, but then she heard Connor driving up and she went to meet him at the door.

He came in smiling. "They loved it," he announced. "People were asking for our card and I was handing them out like crazy."

She put her head to the side and raised her eyebrows as she listened to him. *"Our" card?* When had that happened? But she could deal with that later. Right now she had something else on her mind.

"Now do you want to explain what happened to the crib?"

"Oh." His face changed and suddenly he looked like a boy with a frog in his pocket. "Sure. I, uh, I had to turn it upside down."

"So I see."

He gave her a guilty smile. "Are they okay?"

She nodded. "Sound asleep."

"Good." He looked relieved. "That was the goal."

"But Connor…"

"They wouldn't stay in the cribs," he told her earnestly. "They kept climbing out. And that was just so dangerous. This was the only thing I could think of on the fly. And luckily, they loved it when I put them into their own special cage. I told them to be monkeys and they played happily until they went to sleep. Didn't they?"

"I guess so, but…"

"If I hadn't done it, they would still be climbing out and running for the hills. And we wouldn't have finished in time."

"Okay." She held up a hand and her gaze was steely. "Enough. I understand your logic. What I don't understand is how you could do such a crazy thing without consulting me first."

That stopped him in his tracks. He watched

her and realized she was right. He thought he was doing what was best for her, but without her consent, it was really just what was best for him. He had no right to decide for her. They were her kids.

He'd goofed again and it pained him. Why was he always putting his foot in it where she was concerned? He had to apologize. He swallowed hard. That wasn't an easy thing to do. Taking a deep breath, he forced himself to do what had to be done.

"Jill, you're absolutely right," he said sincerely. "And I'm really sorry. I was wrong to take your agreement for granted. I won't do that again."

Now she had a lump in her throat. Few had ever said that sort of thing to her before, especially not a man. Could she even imagine Brad saying such a thing? Hardly. She felt a small sense of triumph in her chest. She'd asked for an apology and she got one. Wow.

"I guess the first order of business is to figure

out how to make a crib they can't climb out of," she noted, looking at him expectantly.

He feigned astonishment. "Who? Me? You want me to build a crib they can't climb out of?"

"Either that, or come up with a plan," she said, teasing him flirtatiously. "Aren't you here to help?"

His grin was endearingly crooked and he pulled her to him, looking down like a man who was about to kiss a very hot woman. She looked up at him, breath quickening, and she realized she really wanted that kiss. But a look of regret and warning flashed in his eyes. He quickly released her and turned away.

"You ready for that glass of wine now?" he asked, walking toward the wet bar at the end of the room.

She took a deep breath and closed her eyes before she answered. "Sure," she said. "Why not?"

He poured out two crystal glasses of pinot noir and they sat in the living room on a small couch. There was a gentle rain falling and they could see it through the huge glass windows that covered one side of the room.

"What a day," he said, gazing at her as he leaned back in his corner of the couch. The dim light left the wine in their glasses looking like liquid rubies. "It feels like it must have lasted at least a day and a half."

"Or maybe three and a half," she agreed. "And a few shocks to the system." She sighed. "But you came through like a trooper. I couldn't have done it without you."

"I'm glad I was here to help."

She met his gaze and then looked away too quickly. She felt her cheeks reddening and groaned inside. There was nothing to be embarrassed about. Why had she avoided his eyes like that? She coughed to cover up her feelings.

"So tell me the story of this cooking talent you seem to have discovered in the mysterious East," she said quickly.

He grinned. "So you can see the evidence of

my expertise in my work even here," he said grandly.

The corners of her mouth quirked. "No, but you told me you were good, so I believe it."

"Ah." He nodded. "Well, it's all the fault of a young chef named Sharon Wong. We dated each other for most of the last year in Singapore. She taught me everything I know." He made a comical face. "Of course, that was only a small fraction of what *she* knows, but it was a start."

A woman was behind it all. She should have known. But it gave her a jolt. Connor had never seemed to have a special woman in his life. Lots of women, but no one special. Had that changed?

"A chef. Great. I'm partial to chefs. What kind of cuisine?"

"She specializes in Mandarin Chinese but she mostly taught me French basics. She claims every chef needs French cooking as a standard, a baseline to launch from. Sort of like learning Calculus for science classes."

She nodded. "That's why it's so important for Trini to go to the school she just left to attend. She'll get a great grounding in the basics."

He watched her for a moment, then asked, "Why didn't you ever go there?"

She shrugged and stretched back against the pillows, beginning to feel her body relax at last. "I took classes locally, but nothing on that level." Her smile was wistful. "Funny. I applied a few years ago. I got accepted on my first try. A scholarship and everything. But I didn't get to go."

"Why not?"

She gave him a bemused smile. "I married Brad instead."

"Wow, that was a bad decision." He looked pained at the thought. "You gave up going to the school of your dreams to marry Brad?"

"Yes." She threw him a reproving look. He was getting a little adamant about her life choices. "And I do regret it. So that's why I won't let her give it up for anything. She's got to go. She'll learn so much."

He was quiet and she wondered what he was thinking about. Something in the look on his face told her it still bothered him to think of her giving up her dream that way and she wasn't sure why he cared.

Everybody had to make choices. Everybody had to give something up now and then. It was part of life.

"I was just thinking about that time we went to San Francisco," she said a few minutes later. "Remember?"

He looked up and his smile completely changed his face. "Sure I remember. You had set up a weekend to celebrate Brad's birthday with a surprise trip to San Francisco and then you ended up taking me instead."

She nodded, still captivated by that smile.

"It was senior year, wasn't it?" he went on. "You got a hotel just off Union Square and tickets to the ballet—or so you said."

She nodded again. "That was my big mistake. Once I told Brad that, he suddenly had somewhere else he had to be that weekend."

She could hardly believe it. What a fool she'd been in those days. "I was so mad, I told him I was going to take you instead. And he said, sure, go ahead."

Connor smiled, recalling that sunny day. He thought he'd died and gone to heaven. He was walking on air when she asked him to go with her.

A whole weekend with Jill and no Brad. He hadn't even cared if it was the ballet. But the beauty of it was, she was just setting up a surprise, because the tickets that she had were for the Giants in Candlestick Park. The ballet thing was just a ruse to tease Brad and the baseball game was supposed to be his big surprise. Instead it was Connor's.

She gazed at him speculatively. "Sometimes when I look back I wonder why I didn't notice."

His heart gave a lurch. What was she reading into his responses? "Notice what?"

She shrugged. "How little Brad actually cared for me."

Oh, that. It had always been obvious to most of those around her. Brad wanted her when he wanted her, but he didn't confine his activities too close to home. Still, looking at her now, he couldn't stand the haunted expression in her eyes. The last thing in the world she should do was beat herself up over the past.

"He cared plenty," he said gruffly. "He wanted you for himself right from the first. Don't you remember?"

She shook her head and gave him a sad smile. "I think you know what I mean. Anyway, we had a great time in San Francisco, didn't we?"

"Yes, we did." He let his head fall back as he thought of it. That trip had planted dreams in his head. You could say he might have been better off without them, but he didn't think so. His feelings for Jill were a part of that time, even if she never knew it.

"Remember that night? We talked until almost dawn, and then we slept until noon."

"Yeah." They had two rooms, but he never went to his own. There were two beds in hers, one for each of them, and he just stayed with her. He never touched her, but he sure wanted to.

And best of all, it was on that night that he knew he was ready to try to have a real relationship. He'd spent the first few years in college wary of making any sort of commitment to any girl. His background had argued strenuously against it.

But Jill was different. He made up his mind that night that he was going to tell her how he felt about her once they got back to the university. And he was resolved—he was going to take her away from Brad. Somehow, someway, he would do it. He spent hours going over what he wanted to say, how he wanted to make her understand his feelings.

And then they got back to school, and there was Brad on crutches. He'd gone waterskiing and broken his leg. Suddenly he needed Jill. Connor felt himself fading into the background, like some sort of invisible man, and wondering why his timing was always so bad.

It was shortly afterward that he signed up to go to Europe for a semester. When he got back, he learned that Jill and Brad had broken up just after he left. From what he could see, Brad was busy dating every pretty girl on campus while Jill was busy trying to pretend she didn't care.

He took her to his favorite little Italian restaurant and they ate pasta and talked for hours. He ended up with his arm around her while she cried on his shoulder about how awful Brad was being to her. He restrained himself. He was going to do it right. He was going to take it one step at a time.

But once again, the timing wasn't in his favor.

By the next afternoon, Brad was back in her life and all was forgiven.

That was when he'd hardened his heart. It had happened to him one too many times. He wasn't going to let it happen again—ever. Even today he was wary. What seemed like the opportunity to strike so often ended up as the chance to fall on his face instead. It wasn't worth it.

"I think of that trip to San Francisco as an island of happiness in an ocean of stress," she said softly. She looked at him with gentle speculation and a touch of pure affection. "Everything is always so easy with you. And it was always so hard with Brad."

Really? Really?

He stared at her, wondering how she could say such a thing. If that was so, why had she married the hard guy? He was tempted to come right out and ask her that question. That just might clarify a lot of things between them. But before he could think of a way to put it, she spoke again.

"So, was it serious?" she asked him.

He was startled. "Was what serious?"

"You and Sharon Wong?"

"Oh." He laughed, then considered for a moment. "Who knows? It might get to be. If I go back to Singapore."

She turned away. Why did she have such a sick feeling in the pit of her stomach? Was she jealous? Ridiculous. He deserved to fall in love. He deserved some happiness. Hadn't she just been counseling him to find someone to marry? And now she was going to go all green-eyed over a woman he obviously had some affection for? What a fool she was acting.

Connor was probably the best man she knew. He'd always been there for her—except when he took off for places like Singapore. Still, he'd always been a playboy in so many ways. She couldn't imagine him in love.

"I never knew any of your girlfriends in college," she noted. "Why was that? You never showed up with a girl on your arm. I knew they existed, because I heard about them. How come you never brought them around?"

He gazed at her and didn't know what to say. He'd dated plenty of girls in college. But why would he take any of them to meet the one girl he cared about above all others? They would have seen through his casual act in no time.

Funny that she never did.

He stared at her for a long, pulsing moment. "You could have had me anytime you wanted me," he said in a low, rough voice.

There. He'd said it. Finally a little hunk of truth thrown out into this sea of making everyone feel good about themselves. What was she going to do about it?

"Connor!"

She didn't seem to want to take it as truth. More like teasing. Did she really think he was making a joke?

"Be serious," she said, waving that away. "You know that's not true. You didn't want anyone to be your steady girl. You wanted fun and excitement and games and flirting. You didn't want a real relationship. You admitted it at the time." She made a face at him. "You have to realize that back then, what you wanted didn't seem to have anything to do with what I wanted."

He shook his head sadly. "I don't know how you could have read me so wrong."

"I didn't." She made a face at him. "You just don't remember things the way they really were. I was looking for the tie that binds, just like a lot of women at that age. It's a natural instinct. Nesting. I felt a deep need for a strong male, someone to build the foundation of a family with."

He almost rolled his eyes at her. Was she really so self-delusional? "So you chose a guy who didn't want kids."

Her shoulders sagged. He got her on that one. What had she been thinking? He was right. She'd known from the first that he didn't want children. Somehow she had buried that fact under everything, pretending to herself that it didn't matter. Maybe she wouldn't want children, either. Or, more likely, he would change his mind. After all, once it was a clear possibility, surely he would think twice and begin to waver. After all, he loved her. Didn't he?

"I didn't say I chose wisely." She hated to face it, but he had hit the nail on the head. Her mistakes had been easy to avoid, if she'd only been paying more attention. Sighing, she rose. "I want to check on the kids. And I think I'll change out of this uniform. Will you still be up or should I not come back and let you get some sleep?"

He looked at her and realized he wanted her back above all else. He wanted her in his bed, in his arms, in his life. But for now he would have to do with the minimum.

"Sure, come on back," he said, holding up his wineglass. "I've still got a long way to go."

She was glad he'd said that. As she stopped in to look at her sleeping children, she sighed. The upturned crib was not a long-term solution.

Something would have to give. She only hoped it wasn't her peace of mind.

She stopped by the guest room where she slept and changed into something more comfortable, then hurried back down, wondering if he would be asleep before she got back. But he was still staring at the light through his wine and he smiled to welcome her as she entered the room.

She flopped down on the little couch, sitting much closer this time. She was drawn to his warmth, drawn to his masculinity. Might as well face it. She loved looking at him, loved the thought of touching him. Would he kiss her good-night? That would be worth a little loss of sleep.

"Connor, how come I don't really know any-thing about your childhood? How come you never talk about it?"

He took a long sip of wine and looked at her through narrowed eyes. Then he put on his Sam Spade tough-guy voice. "It's not a pretty story, sweetheart. Full of ugliness and despair.

You don't want to worry your pretty little head over it."

"Be serious for a moment," she asked. "Really. I want to know you better."

"Why? What more can there be? We've known each other for more than ten years and suddenly you don't know me?"

"Exactly. You've used our friendship as cover all this time. And now I want to know the truth. What were your parents really like? Not the cartoon version you dredge up for jokes. The real people."

He appeared uncomfortable for a moment, then thought for a second or two, and began.

"Let's just put it this way. As they say in the head-shrinking crowd, I've had lifelong relationship commitment problems, which can probably be traced back to my childhood environment."

"And that means?"

He stared at her. Did she really want him to go there? Okay.

"I learned early and firsthand just what kind of power women have," he said softly. "I watched my mother purposefully drive my father crazy. Payback, I think, for never making as much money as she felt she needed."

"Ouch." She frowned.

"Yes." He glanced at his ruby-red wine and thought back. "My father was a sweet guy in many ways. He tried hard to please her. But he just didn't have what it took to bring in a high salary, and she rubbed his nose in it every day."

"Oh, Connor," she said softly.

"I watched him go through all sorts of contortions to find some little way to bring a smile to her face, but that was virtually impossible. She nitpicked everything. Nothing was ever good enough for her." He threw her a lopsided grin. "Especially me."

"So she nitpicked you, too?"

"Oh, yeah. I think finding something to make me stammer out 'gee, I'm sorry, Mom,' was what made her day for her." He looked at her.

"So I avoided going home. I hung around school in the afternoon, joined every sports team, every debating society, every club that would give me a place to hang out." His gaze darkened. "Meanwhile my father drank himself to death."

"Oh, Connor. I'm so sorry."

He nodded. "It was a waste, really. He was a smart guy. He should have had a better life."

"Yes."

He gazed at her levelly, wondering if he really wanted to get into the next level of this discussion. Did he want to cut a vein and just let it bleed all over the night? Not really. But he might as well explain a little more about why he'd been the way he was when they were younger.

"You know, for years I really was leery of having a relationship with a woman that lasted more than twenty minutes. It just didn't seem worth the risk from what I'd seen."

She wrinkled her nose at him, as if she thought he was being silly. Still, he plowed on.

"But I have a new perspective on it now. I spent the last eighteen months or so in Singapore working with a great guy name George who is married to a wonderful woman named Peggy. I lived in their house and saw their entire interaction, and it helped me understand that decent, loving relationships are possible. I had to look harder at myself and wonder if I had what it takes to have that. I mean, it may be possible, but is it possible for me?"

Jill stared at him. She'd had no idea he had such deep misgivings about lifetime relationships. It made her want to reach out to him, to hold his hand and reassure him. There were plenty of women in the world who didn't treat men the way his mother had. Didn't he know that?

"And what did you decide?" she asked tentatively.

He flashed her a quick grin. "The verdict isn't in yet."

She started to argue about that, but she stopped herself. How could she wrestle him out of opinions that had developed from real life experiences? She didn't have as many bad ones as he did. Maybe it got harder as they piled up.

"Where's your mother now?" she asked.

He shrugged. "I'm not sure. I think she moved to Florida to live with her sister, but we don't keep in touch."

She thought that was a mistake, but she held her tongue. Maybe later she would try to talk to him about how much could be lost when you lost your parents. Instead of going into it directly, she decided to tell him about her background.

"Here's what happened to me," she said. "And Sara. When my mother was alive, we were a happy family. At least, that's the way I remember it. But my father's second marriage was a horror show right from the beginning. That's why Sara and I never warmed to our step-mother, Lorraine." She shook her head.

"She was such a terrible choice for him. And it probably didn't help the marriage that we couldn't like her. He was a good guy, gentle, warm. And she was a shrew."

"Wow," he said, somewhat taken aback. He wasn't used to such strong disapproval from Jill. "That's a pretty negative judgment on the woman."

She shrugged. "Of course, I saw the whole thing through the perspective of a child who had lost her mother and found her father bringing home a new, updated version that didn't please her at all. We were very resentful and probably didn't give her much of a chance, especially after she had a baby. Little Kelly was cute, but it didn't make up for Lorraine. And she didn't like us any better than we liked her and she made it pretty obvious."

"Little Kelly is the one who died last week in a car crash?"

She nodded. "The one I wish we'd been kinder to." She shrugged, but her eyes were sad and haunted. "Too late now." She looked at him again. "And that's what I want you to think about. Don't wait until it's too late to contact your mother again."

He gave her a quizzical look. "Okay. Point taken."

She nodded, then yawned. He smiled.

"You look like a sleepy princess."

She'd traded in her uniform for a short fuzzy robe over the long lacy white nightgown and she looked adorable to him.

"What?" she said, laughing.

"In that gown thing. Even with the little robe over it. You look like you should be in a castle."

She was blushing. Connor had a way of letting her know how pretty he thought she was and she was so hungry for that, it almost brought tears to her eyes.

She smiled back. "I guess we'd better go to bed."

"You're right. We need sleep. I'm only glad we survived the day."

He rose and turned to pull her up beside him and he didn't let go of her hands once they were standing face-to-face, looking at each other.

"I'm glad you came back," she told him, her breath catching in her throat as her pulse began to race. Was he going to kiss her? Or was she going to have to do it herself?

"Me, too." His eyes went so dark, they could have been black instead of blue. He leaned closer, pulling her body up hard against his. "Jill…" he began, and at the same moment, the cell phone in his pocket began to vibrate.

She felt it right away. Sharply drawing in her breath, she stepped back and looked at him. He pulled the phone out, looking for a place to set it down. She reached out and took it from him. Flipping it up, she glanced at the screen and handed it back to him.

"Message for you," she said, and her voice showed no emotion. "How interesting. It's

Brad." Her face didn't reveal a thing, but her eyes were strangely hooded as she turned away and started for the stairs. "Good night," she said over her shoulder.

He cringed, though he wouldn't show it. He stuck the phone back in his pocket and didn't answer it. He hadn't been answering Brad's calls all day. Why should he start now?

But he wished she hadn't seen that.

CHAPTER EIGHT

SLEEPING ON THE couch was getting old fast. Connor stretched and hit the armrest before he had his legs out straight.

"Ouch," he muttered grumpily, wondering why he was awake so early when he was still so tired. Then he noticed the problem. The twins were running around the furniture and yelling at the top of their lungs. He groaned. He really preferred a normal alarm clock.

He opened his eyes just enough to see them. They were pretty cute. But loud. He was going to have to give up any chance for more sleep. He stretched again.

"Great game, kids," he told them groggily, swinging his legs over the side of the couch and sitting up with a yawn.

The boys stopped and stared at him. He stared

back. Tanner pretended to bark like a puppy. Timmy made a sound like a growling monster. He shook his head. They wanted him to respond. He could tell. And he couldn't resist.

Just like the day before, he burst up off the couch, waving the covers to make himself look huge, and gave them a monster growl they wouldn't soon forget.

They screamed with scared happiness and charged out of the room, pushing and shoving to both fit through the door at once.

Jill came in and glared at him. "They won't be able to eat their breakfast if you rile them up too much," she warned.

He waved his sheet-covered arms at her and growled. She shook her head and rolled her eyes.

"How come you're not scared?" he complained.

"Because you look so ridiculous," she told him. She laughed softly, letting her gaze slide over his beautiful body. What on earth did he do in Singapore that kept him so fit? His muscles were hard and rounded and tan and a lot of that was on display. His chest was all male and his pajama bottoms hung low on his hips. He took her breath away.

"But you do look cute as a scary monster," she allowed, trying to avoid an overdose of his sexiness by looking away. "We might be able to use your skills at Halloween."

"Hey, no fair," he said as he looked her over sleepily. "You already changed out of your princess dress."

"I'm going incognito for the day," she told him. "They don't let princesses bake Bundt cakes."

"They should."

"I know." She smiled at him then asked with false cheerfulness, "What did Brad want last night?"

He shrugged. "I didn't answer it."

She stared at him for a moment, then looked away. "I just checked my email. There are already two more orders from people who had cake last night. That makes four who want their cakes today, and two more for the weekend."

"I said you had star power. Didn't I?"

She reached out to take the sheet from him and he leaned forward and dropped a quick kiss on her mouth before she could draw back. She looked up into his eyes and the room began to swim around her.

"They should let princesses do whatever they want," he said softly, and then he reached out and pulled her closer and she slipped her arms around his neck and his mouth found hers.

Finally!

She'd been waiting for this kiss forever—or anyway, it seemed that way. She melted in his arms, taking in his taste and letting her body feel every hard part of him it could manage. His rounded muscles turned her on and his warm, musky smell sent her senses reeling.

And then the doorbell rang.

She collapsed against him, laughing and shaking her head. "Why does fate hate me?" she protested.

He held her close and buried his face in her hair, then let her go.

A timer went off.

"Oh, no, I've got to check that," she said.

"I'll go to the door," he offered.

"Really?" She looked at him skeptically, wondering who was going to get a stunning view of that magnificent chest and hoping it wasn't the church people. Then she rushed on into the kitchen to check her cake.

It definitely needed to come out. She set it on the cooling rack and looked around at the mess that still existed from yesterday. She usually made it a practice never to go to bed with a dirty pan left in the sink, but she'd broken that rule last night. Now she had a couple of counters full of pans that needed washing. She was working on that when Connor came into the kitchen.

"Who's at the door?" she asked distractedly.

Connor made a face. "The Health Department Inspector."

She turned to stare at him. "What? He just came last week."

He shrugged. "I guess he's back."

And so he was, coming into the kitchen and looking around with massive disapproval all over his face. Tall and thin, he wore glasses and had a large, fluffy mustache, along with a pinched look, that made him look like a bureaucratic force to be reckoned with.

Connor made a face at her and left to put on some clothes. The inspector sniffed at him as he left, then looked back at the kitchen.

"What the hell is going on here?" he demanded, looking at the pot and pan strewn counters.

Jill had a smart-alecky answer right on the tip of her tongue, but she held it back. This was the health inspector. He could ruin her if he wanted to. Shut her down. She had to be nice to him, much as it stuck in her craw.

"Look, this is such a bad time for you to show up. Unannounced, I might add. Aren't you supposed to make appointments?"

He glared at her. "Aren't you supposed to be ready at all times for inspection?"

She gave him a fake smile. "Sorry about the mess. I'm in the middle of cleaning it up. We had a huge, huge day yesterday. Things will be back in order in no time."

"That would be wise," he said. "I wouldn't want to have to write you up for kitchen contamination."

She gaped at him in outrage. "There's clutter, there's mess, but there's no contamination. Please!"

He shrugged, then turned as Connor reappeared, dressed in the same shirt and slacks he'd been wearing for three days now.

"What are you doing here?" he asked.

"Moral support," Connor responded simply. "I'm just a friend. I'm helping."

His eyes narrowed. "Helping how?"

Connor shrugged, instinctively knowing this might be a time to be careful and wary. "Odd jobs. Deliveries."

"Ah." He appeared skeptical. "Let's hope you aren't doing any of the baking. Because if you are, you're going to need to be screened for medical conditions. You'll need a blood test. And more. We don't want you touching the food if you're not healthy. Your papers must be in order."

Connor frowned at the man. "What papers?"

"The ones you need to qualify to do any cooking whatsoever."

Connor sighed and looked away. "Ah, those papers."

"Yes. Records of shots and tests, etc. Medical problems in the last ten years. You understand."

Connor made a face, but he said as pleasantly as possible, "Of course."

The man glared at him. "So? Where are your papers?"

"Really?" Connor said, beginning to get belligerent. "Hey, Mr. Health Inspector, let's see *your* papers."

The man produced a badge and a license and Connor stared at them, realizing he had no idea if they were authentic or not. But he was beginning to have his doubts about this guy.

Jill winced. Connor looked about ready to do something that would jeopardize her business and she had to stop him. Standing behind the inspector, she shook her head and put her finger to her lips, then jerked her thumb toward the other room. Connor hesitated, then followed her out into the hallway, leaving the inspector to poke around at will.

"Connor, don't antagonize him, for heaven's sake," she whispered. "He'll probably write me up for some little thing and then he'll have to come back to check if I've fixed it. But at least he'll go. So leave him alone."

Connor was frowning. "How often does this guy show up here?" he asked her.

"Too much if you ask me. I almost feel like it's

harassment at this point. And the funny thing is, every time he comes, something seems to go wrong. I don't know if it's just that I get nervous and then I don't keep focused on what I'm doing or what."

Connor's gaze narrowed. "What sort of things go wrong?"

"Oh…one time the oven wouldn't work anymore and I had to get a repairman out. Another time somehow the refrigerator got unplugged and it was hours before we knew it. A lot of supplies spoiled and I had to throw them out."

"No kidding." He frowned. "Is he the same official who comes every time?"

"No. But he does come the most. And he says the goofiest things. In fact, I called the health department to complain about him a few weeks ago. They claimed they hadn't sent anyone."

Connor's face was hard as stone. "That doesn't seem right."

"I know. But what can I do? I don't dare confront him. What if he pulls my license?"

Connor shook his head. "Jill, I don't buy it for a minute."

She stared at him. "What do you mean?"

"I think he's a phony. He's got to go."

"What?" She grabbed at his arm to stop him, but he pulled away and marched back into the kitchen, catching the stranger with a tiny camera in his hand.

"Get the hell out of here," he told the inspector in a low, furious voice.

"Connor!" Jill cried, coming in behind him. "You can't talk that way to the inspector!"

But the man seemed to take Connor quite seriously. He raised his hands as though to show he didn't mean any harm and said, "Okay, okay. Take it easy. I'm going."

And he turned around and left as quickly as he could.

Jill stared after him, then looked at Connor. "What the heck?" she cried.

He turned and gave her a look. "Jill, that man's not a real health inspector. Can't you see that?"

"No." She blinked in bewilderment. "What is he then?"

"A private investigator pretending to be a health inspector."

"But why would…?" Her face cleared. "Brad!"

Connor nodded. "That's my guess."

She sank into a chair. "Oh, my gosh. I can't believe that. Brad sent him to spy on me."

"And to sabotage your business, I would guess."

She closed her eyes and took a deep breath. "Why didn't I think of that? I knew there was something fishy about the way he kept showing up." She looked up at Connor. "I should have known."

But Connor was still thinking things over. "Okay, I'm ready to believe that was Brad at work. So the question is, what else has he been meddling in?"

She thought for a moment, then put a hand over her mouth. "Oh, my gosh." She grabbed his hand and held it tightly. "Connor, I don't know this for sure, but I was told that Brad tried to get them to disallow my license. Right at the beginning."

He lowered himself into the chair beside her, still holding her hand. "Why would he do that?"

"Well, he never wanted me to keep this house. He thought I ought to move to the mainland and get an apartment, put the kids in day care and get a regular job. He sort of acted like he thought I was trying to extort money from him by doing anything else."

His face was cold as granite. "Tell me more."

"It took a while to get started. At first, I didn't have any of the right equipment. I used every penny I got from Brad to help pay for the commercial oven, but I still needed to buy a three-unit sink and the special refrigeration I needed. When he found out what I was doing, he was furious."

"And stopped giving you money," he guessed.

She nodded. "Pretty much. Which only made

it more important that I find a way to grow my business." She laced her fingers with his.

"You know, you hit a place where you can either move forward, or settle for something less, and get stuck in that great big nowhere land." She sighed. "In order to get to where I might make some actual profit, I had to take the chance. I needed funding. So…"

She met his gaze and looked guilty. "So, yes, I took out a loan so that I could finish buying the supplies I needed."

"What did you use to get a loan? The house?"

She nodded. "That's why it's so scary that this house is still underwater and they won't give me a mortgage modification."

"You've tried?"

"Countless times."

"You're in a tight spot."

She nodded. "I'm standing at the edge of the cliff, you mean. And the ground is starting to crumble under my feet."

His free hand took her chin and lifted her face

toward his, then he leaned in and kissed her softly. "I'll catch you," he said, his voice husky. "I'm here, Jill. I won't let you hit the rocks."

She smiled, loving his generous spirit, but not really believing his words. How could he stop the chain of events that seemed to be overwhelming her? It wasn't likely. They'd had a good day yesterday and he'd made that possible. But goodwill—and cake sales—could only go so far. Every step forward seemed to bring on two steps back. She was beginning to lose hope.

He hesitated, then shook his head and drew back from her. "Okay, here's what I don't understand. This just really gets to me. Why do you let Brad still be such a huge part of your life?"

"I…I don't."

"Yes, you do. You're divorced. He's not even giving you the money you should be getting for the kids. He doesn't want anything to do with the children." He frowned, searching her eyes. "Why let him affect you in any way? Why maintain any ties at all?"

She blinked. It was hard to put this in words. How to explain how alone she felt in the world? In some ways, Brad was still her only lifeline. It was too scary to cut that off.

"The only real, legal ties we still have is the business," she said instead of trying to explain her emotional connection to her past. "I still own fifteen percent of it."

He nodded. He knew that. "Do you have a voting position on the board?"

She shrugged. "I'm not really sure if I do or not. I think I'm supposed to but I've never tried to use it. I suppose I should ask a lawyer."

"At the very least."

"The only reason I keep it, to tell you the truth, is that emotionally, I just can't give up on it yet. It's still a part of my life, a part of my past, all those years we spent building it into the enterprise it is today."

He nodded. Did that answer the question? Her ties to Brad were still too strong. But were they that way from fear…or love? Hard to pull those two apart for analysis. And the answer to that meant everything.

Connor was so angry inside, both at Brad and at himself, he couldn't stay near her for now. Instead he went out and walked down to the ferry and then around the quaint little village and back again. He finally had something he wanted to say to Brad, but when he tried calling him, he found his old pal had turned the tables, and now he wasn't taking calls from Connor.

Voice mail was his only recourse. He waited for the beep.

"Hey, Brad. I just wanted to let you know that I know the health inspector is a phony. He's someone who works for you. If he comes here again, I'll have him arrested for impersonating a government employee.

"About those shares. If you really want them so badly, why don't you come and ask her for them like a man? Why don't you face her? And why don't you offer her something real? You never know what might happen.

"In the meantime, other than that, leave Jill alone. Go live your own life and forget about hers."

He clicked off and tried to tame the rage that roiled in him. Jill didn't deserve any of this. He only hoped she would let him stay here to help her get out from under all this. He knew she couldn't get Brad out of her system, but there wasn't much he could do about that. He didn't care about his own emotional involvement anymore. So, he was probably going to get his heart broken. So what? His love for Jill was too strong to try to deny any longer. And all he wanted was what was good for her. He had to stay.

When he walked into the house, he heard Jill singing in the kitchen. He had to stop for a moment and listen, marveling at her. What was she, some kind of angel? Whatever—she was everything he knew he wanted. And would probably never have.

"Hey," he told her as he came up behind her,

putting his arms around her. She leaned back into him and smiled. "I'm getting pretty funky in these clothes," he said. "I think I'll run into town and get some fresh things from the hotel room. Can I bring anything back for you?"

She turned in his embrace and kissed him. "Just bring yourself back. That's all I need," she said.

He kissed her again and the kiss deepened. The way he felt about her grew every time he touched her. Right now, it seemed like fireworks going off in his chest. This was the way he wished it could always be.

Jill stood at the sliding glass door looking out at the grassy hill that was her backyard. Connor was outside playing with the twins, chasing them up and down the hill, laughing, picking up one and then the other to whirl about and land gently again. Her heart was full of bittersweet joy. Tears trembled in her eyes.

If only Brad could be this way. If he really

met the boys, if he tried to get to know them, wouldn't he realize how wonderful they were? Wouldn't he have to love them? Wouldn't that make everything better?

As she watched, Connor fell, iron-cross style, into a huge bed of leaves, and the boys raced each other to jump on top of him. She could hear the laughter from where she was behind glass and it answered her own questions.

No. Brad would never love the boys, because he didn't want to. He wouldn't let himself. It was time she faced facts.

She heard the front door open and she turned that way.

"Jill!"

"In here, Sara." She frowned. Her sister's voice sounded high and strained. What had happened now?

Sara appeared, looking a little wild. "Did you get the letter?"

"What letter?"

"From Social Services." She waved an official-looking envelope. "Did you get one, too?"

"I don't know. Connor brought in the mail. I think he left it on the entryway table. Let me get it."

She stepped into the foyer and found the envelope Sara was talking about. Connor and the boys were coming back into the family room as she returned to it. The boys were jumping around him like puppies.

"I promised them ice cream," he said after nodding at Sara. "I'm hoping you actually have some."

"Don't worry." Jill put the envelope down and went into the kitchen. They all followed her and she pulled two Popsicles out of the freezer for them. "They'll accept this as a substitute," she said. "Now go on out and play in the sunroom. I don't care if you drip all over that floor."

They did as they were told, dancing happily on their toes. Connor laughed as he watched them go, then looked at Jill. They shared a secret smile.

Sara groaned. "Come on. Open the mail. You won't believe this."

"What does it say?"

"You need to read it for yourself. Go ahead. Read it. I'll wait."

Connor looked at Sara and said, "Hey, you look really upset."

Her eyes flashed his way. "Did Jill tell you about our stepsister? She died in a car accident last week."

"Yes, she did tell me. I'm sorry."

Sara nodded, then looked at Jill, waiting.

Moments later, Jill handed the letter to Connor and he noticed right away that her fingers were trembling. She turned and looked at her sister, wide-eyed. "I don't believe it."

Sara nodded, looking flushed. "Told you."

Connor glanced at the letter. It seemed to be about someone named Kelly Darling. Then he connected the name. It was the stepsister who had died the week before. Kelly Darling. It seemed that Kelly had a baby. A three-month-old baby. Jill and Sara were her only living relatives that could be found. Would either of them care to claim the child?

"A baby," he said. "And you didn't know?"

"No." Jill shook her head. "I guess she wasn't married. We hadn't heard from her for so long."

Sara nodded mournfully. "And now, a baby."

Jill felt tears threatening again. "Poor little thing."

Sara flashed her a look. "Kelly's baby." She shook her head. "I don't think we've seen Kelly more than three times in the last fifteen years."

"And that's our fault," Jill said mournfully. "We should have made more of an effort."

Sara shrugged. "Why? She never liked us. The last time I saw her, she was furious with me."

Jill looked surprised. "What happened?"

"She wanted to borrow five thousand dollars

to help pay for a certification class she wanted to take."

"Some kind of computer class?"

"No. It was to qualify as a professional dog trainer. When I pointed out that I didn't see how she was going to be able to pay me back on the salaries beginning dog trainers make, she told me I was ruining her life and she never wanted to see me again."

Jill sighed. "Well, she was an awfully cute little baby."

Sara looked at Jill and bit her lip. "I'm sure they'll find some relative we don't even know about to take the child."

Jill frowned. "Maybe. But…"

"Jill!" Sara cried. "Don't you dare! There is no way you can take on another baby."

Jill looked pained. "What about you?" she asked.

"Me?" Sara's face registered shock. It was obvious that option hadn't even entered her mind. "Me?" She shook her head strenuously. "I don't do babies. I can barely manage to watch your little angels for more than an hour without going mad."

"Sara, she's our flesh and blood. She's our responsibility."

"How do you figure that? I don't see it. She was Kelly's responsibility, and now they'll find someone to adopt her. Tons of people want babies that age."

Jill was shaking her head. "I don't know...."

Sara groaned and looked tortured. Stepping closer, she took her sister's hands in her own. "Jill, I haven't come right out and told you this. I've tried to hint it, just to prepare you, but... I'm going to be moving down to Los Angeles. And my job is going to include almost constant travel, especially to New York. There's no room for a baby in that scenario." She had tears sliding down her cheeks. "And that also means I won't be here to help you. You can't even begin to think of taking this baby."

Jill looked at her and didn't say a thing.

Connor watched her. She was going to take the baby. He could tell. He tried to understand the dynamics here. This was another blow to Jill, another obstacle in her struggle to survive. And yet, that wasn't the way she was taking it. She didn't look at it as the end of her hopes and dreams, a financial and emotional disaster. She was seeing it as another burdensome responsibility, but one that she would accept. He'd known her for years but he'd never realized how deep her strength went. Where had that come from? Where had she found the capacity to take on everyone else's problems? Was being the oldest sister the key? Or was it just the way her soul was put together?

"They'll find a good home for the baby somewhere, I'm sure," Sara was insisting. "Don't they have agencies to do things like that?"

Jill frowned. That just wasn't right and she knew it. "Sara…"

Sara closed her eyes and turned away.

"I've got to go. I'm expecting half a dozen

calls and I've got to prepare myself." She looked back and hesitated, then said with fierce intensity, "Jill, you can't be considering taking that baby. I won't let you."

Jill winced. She knew what was going to happen. It was inevitable. She couldn't expect Sara to understand. Babies…life…family—that was what she'd been put on earth to deal with. So Brad hadn't worked out. Too bad. So her cake business was trembling on the brink and might just crumble. Okay. But turn down taking care of a baby? Her father's grandchild? Her own niece? No. Impossible. If Sara couldn't face it, that baby had only one chance.

She followed Sara to the door and touched her arm before she could escape. "Sara, I'm going to call them. I want that baby here with us."

A look of abject terror flared in her sister's eyes. Slowly, she shook her head, her lower lip trembling. "You're crazy," she whispered. "Jill, I beg you. Don't do it." And then she turned on her heel and hurried to her car.

Jill came back into the house and went straight to Connor as though drawn by a magnet.

"Are you sure?" he asked her.

"About the baby?" She smiled. "Yes. There is no way I could let Kelly's baby go to strangers. I'm going to get in touch with these people right away. The sooner we get her here the better."

"Jill, your heart is definitely in the right place. But can you do it? You're already overextended. You're on the ragged edge with these two little boys. Can you take on another child like this?"

"I have no choice. I couldn't live with myself if I didn't do it."

His heart was overflowing with love for her, and he knew what she was doing courted disaster. His brain told him Sara was right, but his heart—it was all for Jill. "Come here. I have to hold you. You are so special…"

"Oh, Connor." She started to cry and he held her while she sobbed in his embrace. "It's scary, but it's wonderful, too. It's the right thing to do."

"I just hope it won't be too much for you," he said, kissing her tears away.

She kissed him back. "Sometimes I feel like I'm at my breaking point, but something always comes through to save the day. And right now, it's your arms around me. Connor, I'm so glad you're here."

And she started to sob again. He held her close, enjoying the feel of her and the sweet, fruity scent from her hair. He loved her and he would be there for her as long as she let him stay. But deep inside, he knew a time would come when she would want him to leave. He was prepared for that. He only hoped it didn't come for a long, long time.

CHAPTER NINE

AN HOUR LATER, Jill invited Connor to help her take the boys to the park to play on the swings and in the sandbox. They took little shovels and pails and made the trek on foot, through the residential streets and over the low-lying berm that marked the edge of the park area. The boys ran ahead, then came back for protection when dogs barked or a car came on the end of the street. Then they reached the park and the twins were in heaven.

When they tired of the swings, they got to work with the shovels, tossing sand and shrieking with happiness. After making a vain attempt to keep order, Jill and Connor sat back and let them play the way that seemed to come naturally to them. There weren't many other children around, so they gave them their freedom.

"I heard from Trini this morning," she told him. "I got an email. She's behind in a few classes, but she thinks she can catch up. She's thrilled to be there." She smiled happily. "She's going to keep me apprised with daily bulletins. That'll be great. It's just like vicariously going myself."

"I wish you could go yourself. We ought to be able to figure out a way...."

"We"? She looked at him sideways. But that seemed like a silly thing to have an argument about, so she moved on.

"So tell me more about what you were doing in Singapore all this time," she said, looking at the way his unruly hair flew around his head, much the way hers did, though his was dark as coal and hers was bright as sunshine. "You told me about the nice couple you lived with and worked for, and you told me about the chef you fell in love with—"

"Whoa! Hold on. I never told you that."

"Really?" Her eyes twinkled with mischief.

"Gee, I don't know where I picked that up. I must have misheard it."

He knocked against her with his shoulder. "Come on, Jill. You know you're the only woman I've ever loved."

"Wow." She pressed closer to him. "It would be nice to think that was true."

He turned his head and said, close to her ear, "Count on it."

There was something in the way he said it that made her look up into his eyes. They were just kidding each other, weren't they?

"So tell me," she said after they sat down at the edge of the play area. She was sifting sand through her fingers. "Are you really going back or not?"

"That depends."

"On what?"

On whether I can make you fall in love with me. On whether you can wipe Brad out of your calculations for your future. On whether you can believe in me.

But he sighed and actually said, "The company got bought out by a huge corporation. George made a fine haul on it. And under our contract, he gave me a nice chunk of change, too. So if I went back, it would be to link up with old George again and work on the next big idea."

She smiled with happy memories. "Just like the three of us did when we started MayDay."

"Exactly."

"Only Brad hasn't been bought out by anyone."

"No. Not yet."

She frowned, thinking that over. "And what are you going to do with your profits?"

He shrugged. "I don't know. Right now I'm pretty much looking around for a company to invest in. Some nice, clean little start-up. Preferably in the food business."

She looked at him suspiciously. "Are you teasing me?"

"Teasing you?" He looked shocked at the concept. "Why would I tease you?"

"Because you love to knock me off balance," she said with mock outrage. "You always have."

He leaned back against the rock behind him and laughed at her. She began to poke him in the ribs.

"You love it. Admit it. You love to have a good giggle over my naïveté. Fess up!"

He laughed harder and she began to tickle him. He grabbed her and pulled her down beside him and kissed her nose, making her laugh, too. And then he kissed her for real and she kissed him back and the warmth spread quickly between them.

"You're like a drug," he whispered, dropping kisses on her face. "I don't dare take too much of you."

"Good thing, too," she whispered back. "Because I only have that little tiny bit to give."

"Liar," he teased, kissing her mouth again.

She sighed, holding back the sizzle that threatened to spill out and make this inappropriately exciting. That would have to wait. But she had no doubt they would be able to explore it a bit more later.

"Hey," she said, pulling back up. "We're supposed to be watching the boys."

Luckily the two toddlers were still enchanted with the pails and shovels. Connor and Jill sat up and shook off the sand and grinned at each other.

"Okay," she said. "Now tell me what you're really going to do with the money."

"Just what I said. I've got my eye on a nice little Bundt cake bakery."

She didn't laugh this time. "No, Connor. I will not take charity from you."

He'd known she would react that way but it didn't hurt to start setting the background and give her a chance to think about it. "I'm talking about investing. I wouldn't put my money anywhere that I didn't expect to make a profit on it."

She was shaking her head adamantly. "I don't have shares to sell. That just won't work and you know it."

No, he didn't know it, but he had known she would be a hard sell on the idea. Hopefully he would have more time to see what he could develop to do for her. "Jill..."

"Connor, I'm still bound to Brad by his company. I refuse to play that game again."

Ouch. That could make all the difference. He nodded slowly, frowning. "Jill, when you say you're still bound to Brad, what do you mean?" He looked her full in the face, searching her eyes for hints of the truth. "Do you still want him back?"

She thought for a moment, then looked at him, clear-eyed. "Connor, for a long time, I wanted Brad back. But not for me. I wanted him back for his children. What will it be like for them to go through life wondering why their father didn't want them? It breaks my heart." Her voice caught and she paused. "For so long, I was so sure, once he saw them, once he held them in his arms…"

He couldn't stand to see her still hoping. He wanted to smash something. Carefully he tried to tell her.

"He's just not made that way, Jill. Brad doesn't want to love a child. He doesn't want to complicate his life like that. He doesn't even want a wife at this point. He thinks he needs to keep the way clear so that he can think big thoughts and make cool-headed decisions. Human relationships only mess things up as far as he's concerned." He shrugged, grimacing. "I don't know why we didn't see that more clearly from the beginning."

"Maybe we did and we just didn't want to believe it."

She closed her eyes. She still had her dreams. She sometimes thought that maybe, if he saw her again, if they did come face-to-face, he would see what he'd once loved in her and realize what he'd lost—and want it back.

No. It wasn't going to happen. She'd given up on that fantasy a long time ago. So why did she still cling to the shards of that relationship?

"When did you start to figure out the truth about Brad?" Connor asked her softly.

Her smile was mirthless. "When I realized he was cheating on me."

He drew his breath in sharply. "You knew?"

She looked at him. "Connor, I'm not stupid. Gullible, maybe. Too weak to stand up for myself when I should, sometimes. But not dumb."

They were silent for a long moment, then Connor asked, "What do you think Brad will say about you taking on another baby?"

She laughed. "Luckily it doesn't matter what he says. Does it?"

The boys were tussling. One was hitting the other with a plastic pail and both were starting to cry. The inevitable end to a lovely time being had by all. Jill and Connor rose from their sitting place and started across the sand to mediate the battle, but on the way, they held hands.

* * *

Jill baked two more cakes once they got home and Connor put the boys down for their naps. They both fell asleep as soon as their heads hit their mattresses. He watched them for a while, amazed at how much he cared for them already. Then he went down to help Jill with the bakery business.

"So what's next?" he asked, sitting at the kitchen table and eating a nice large slice of Strawberry Treat. "What's the plan?"

She glanced back at him as she mixed up a fresh glaze. "Stay out of the way of the inspectors. Obey all regulations scrupulously. Grow my business. Hire some employees and get my own shop." She threw him a smile. "In other words, succeed."

He took another bite and nearly swooned with the deliciousness of it all. "You're the best Bundt cake baker on the island. Probably the best in all of Seattle. But all of Seattle isn't going to come here for their cakes. Your customers are basically the people on this island. Are there enough of them to let you be successful?"

She came to the table and dropped down into a seat across from him. "This is exactly my nightmare question. How can I get a large customer base?"

"And what's your answer?"

She shook her head. "I haven't really dealt with it because I'm scared of what it will take."

"And what is that?"

She frowned. "I have to branch out. I know it. I have to develop a full-blown bakery out of this. I have to make cookies and pies and éclairs and bear-claws and dinner rolls. I have to learn to do everything. It's my only hope."

"And your competition?"

She nodded. "There are two bakeries here, both run by older bakers who are about at the end of their bakery careers, I would think. So there should be room for me." She made a face. "If I can come up to the challenge."

He was impressed that she'd thought this out

so fully. It gave him the reassurance that she really meant to make a go of it. Because she was going to have to work very hard to last.

"You've really developed a good business brain, haven't you?"

"I developed it right next to you. Remember when we used to brainstorm together during the early days at MayDay?"

"I do." He smiled at her. "But how are you going to do all this without someone here to help you? I can't even understand how you've done this much so far."

"It isn't easy."

He thought about that for a moment, then turned back and said, "You're going to have to have some help. Face it."

She nodded. "I know. I'm thinking of giving Mrs. Mulberry another chance."

"Great. I think she deserves it."

"She means well and she wants to do it. So there you go."

He nodded. "If you're with her most of the

time, you can train her. And she'll begin to understand what the twins need. I'm sure it will go well."

She grinned at him. "I never realized what an optimist you are. Just a regular what-me-worry-kid."

"Sure. I learned long ago that being happy is better than being angry all the time."

He watched her work, nursing a cup of coffee and enjoying the smells of a working bakery. It all seemed too quiet and idyllic. Until you remembered that Brad was probably on his way. Most likely he would drive up from Portland. And then he would come here. Connor wanted to be here when he arrived. There was no way he was going to let Jill face him alone.

Jill was chatting about something or other. He wasn't paying much attention. He was too busy enjoying her, smiling at the flour on her face, watching the way her body moved, the way her breasts were swelling just inside the opening of her shirt, those long, silky legs. She'd always been his main crush, but now she was becoming something more. He wanted her and his body was letting him know the need was getting stronger.

From the beginning, it had seemed she was strangely dominated, almost mesmerized, by Brad. She'd been Brad's and he'd been crazy jealous, but he'd never thought he would have a chance with her. Now, he did. It all depended on how strong that bond between them still was.

He had his own bond with her—didn't he? Even if she didn't feel it, he did. She walked out toward where he was sitting at the table, talking about something he wasn't really listening to and stopping near him. Reaching out, he caught her wrist and tugged her closer. She looked down at him, saw the darkness in his eyes, and her own eyes widened, and then her mouth softened and she sank down beside him.

She hadn't hesitated. She'd come to him as soon as she saw he wanted her to. That filled him with a bright new sense of wonder. He wanted to hold her forever, make a declaration, make love to her and make her his own.

He wrapped her in his arms and she sighed as he began to drop small, impatient kisses along the line of her neck. She turned, giving him more access to her body in a way he hadn't expected.

His heart was pounding now, filling him with a sort of excitement he hadn't felt for a long, long time. She was warm and soft and rounded in the best places for it. He kissed just under her ear and suddenly she was turning in his arms, moaning, searching for his mouth with hers, and then that was all there was.

The kiss. It took his breath away at the same time it put his brain into orbit. He couldn't think. He could only feel. And taste. And ache for her.

Jill felt his release, his acceptance of the desire swelling between them, and she was tempted to give way to it as well. She knew this had to stop but for the moment, she couldn't find the strength to make it happen. She hungered for his heat, longed for his touch, moved beneath his hands as though she couldn't get enough of him.

There was no way to stop this feeling. Was it love? Was it loneliness that needed healing? Or was it a basic womanly demand that smoldered deep inside all the time, hidden by the events of the day, and only revealed when the right man touched her?

That was it. She'd known passion before, but this was different. She not only wanted his body, but she also needed his heart and soul, and for once, she thought she just might have a chance to get that.

She was drowning in his kiss. His mouth tasted better than anything she'd ever known. She writhed with it, moaned and made tiny cries as though she could capture the heat and keep it forever in her body. And then reality began to swim back into focus and she tried to pull away.

It wasn't easy. His kisses were so delicious and his hands felt so good. But it had to be done. There were cakes in the oven. There were children waking up from their naps.

Reality. Darn it all.

"Jill," he murmured, his face buried in her curly hair, "we're going to have to find a way to do something about this."

"Are we?" But she smiled. Her body was still resonating with the trembling need for him, and she totally agreed. Somehow, they had to do something about it—soon.

The shadows were longer. Afternoon was flowing into evening. The boys were stirring and Connor went up to supervise their waking. He got them changed and brought them down to play in the playroom, listening as they called back and forth with what seemed like their own special language.

The doorbell rang and he stiffened. He didn't

think Brad could have gotten here this fast unless he flew. But it was a possibility.

He went out into the entryway. It wasn't Brad.
Jill was talking to the mailman and signing for
a certified letter. She closed the door and ripped
the letter open.

"What in the world is this going to be?" she
muttered, her mind on her cakes. Then she
looked at the letter. Frowning, she looked at it
again.

"What does this mean?" she asked Connor.

He glanced over her shoulder and frowned.
"It looks like the bank is calling your loan."

She gasped. "Are they allowed to do that?"

"Let me see the letter." He read it over more
carefully. "Okay, it says here that their investi-
gation has revealed that you have insufficient
security and they don't trust your collateral."
He looked at her. "You used this house, didn't
you?"

She nodded, her eyes wide with alarm.

He went back to the letter. "They also claim

that, if you study your contract, you will find it has a 'Due for Any Reason Clause' which allows them to call the loan without having to justify it." He stared at her in distaste. "Just because they want to." His face darkened as he thought that through. "Or because someone bribes them to do it," he suggested.

She stared at him and then she whispered, "Brad?"

He shrugged. "You probably won't ever be able to prove it."

She took the letter and read it again. That was what it said. Her loan was being called. There was no doubt in her mind that Brad had something to do with this.

She was shaking. Everything she tried to do seemed to fail. She wasn't getting anywhere. It was so hard—it was like running in quicksand. In her worst nightmares, she'd never thought of this. How could he do this to her?

"He won't ever cut me free, will he?" She raised her tragic gaze to Connor's blue one.

"He doesn't want me, but he still wants to manipulate me. He still wants to control my life." Her voice got higher. "Am I doomed to be tied to this man forever? That's like being married without any of the perks. I just have to obey, forget the love and all that other stuff."

Connor took her shoulders and held her firmly.

"Jill, calm down. I know it's frustrating, but maybe if you find out exactly what he thinks he wants."

"Like what? For me to get rid of the boys?" She knew she looked wild. And why not? She felt wild. "You actually think I would consider something like that?"

"No, of course not." He hesitated. "But I don't think that's what he's after right now."

"Really? And why do you know so much about what he's after? Did he tell you?" Her face changed as she realized what she'd said. "That's it, isn't it?" She stared at him. "You know what he wants. You just haven't told me yet."

He had a bad feeling about where this train

of thought was leading. He took a deep breath. "Jill…"

She backed away from him. "Okay, Connor," she said coldly, her face furious. "Are you finally ready to tell me what Brad wants from me? What he sent you to tell me?"

He tried to touch her but she pulled away.

"Tell me," she demanded.

He shook his head, knowing she was in no mood to hear this and think logically. But he didn't have any choice. He had to tell her. He should have done it sooner. But still he hesitated, not sure how to approach it.

"Brad asked me to talk to you," he admitted. "But I never told him I would. And once I saw you again, I knew I would never do his dirty work for him. If he wanted to ask you something he had to come and do it himself."

"I see," she said cynically. At this point, she was ready to believe the worst of anyone and everyone. "So you decided for some reason, I wasn't ready. I wasn't softened up enough.

You decided to go slow. You needed to sweeten me up, flatter me a little, get me ready for the slaughter."

"Jill…" He shook his head, appalled that she would think that.

She drew in a trembling breath. "I can't believe you would gang up on me with Brad this way."

That was like a knife through his heart. "I'm not."

She wasn't listening. "So how about it, Connor? Am I ready now? Are you going to stop lying and tell me the truth?"

He shook his head. He might as well get this over with. "Okay, Jill. What Brad wants is those company shares he gave you when you divorced. He thinks he needs them back."

She looked surprised. "Why?"

He shrugged. "I think he's having a fight with some of the other shareholders. He wants to stop a power play by some who are getting together to outvote him on some company policies."

She pressed her lips together and thought about that for a moment. Then she glared at him again.

"Is that all? Really? Then why didn't you tell me the truth from the beginning?"

He turned away, grimacing. Then he turned back. "I asked you before, Jill, and I'm going to ask you again. You've hinted now and then that you would take Brad back if you could. Do you still feel that way?"

She thought for a moment, pacing from him to the glass door and back again. "What I really want is to have my life back. Do you understand that? I chose Brad to be at my side forever and I gave birth to two angels, two gifts for him." She stared at him with haunted eyes. "So why did he reject them? Why did he reject me and the life we'd both created together? I want that life."

He winced. That wasn't really what he'd wanted to hear.

"I want things to be like they used to be. I want my life back."

"So you still want Brad back."

She didn't answer that.

Who was he to tell her it couldn't happen? Stranger things had.

"Nothing has changed?" he asked her, incredulous.

She shook her head. "Of course. Everything has changed." Anger flashed through her eyes like flames from a fire. "And now you've proven you stand with Brad."

He grimaced. He couldn't let her think he wasn't behind her one hundred percent. "Jill, listen to me. Seeing you again, I realized how much I care for you. How much I missed you and all you've always meant to me. I want you for myself. I don't want Brad to have anything to do with...with our relationship."

She stared at him as though she hadn't heard a word he'd said. "But you've kept in constant contact with him, haven't you? Isn't he always calling on your phone?"

"Yes, but..."

"Connor, you lied to me!"

"No, I didn't. That's ridiculous."

"Yes, you did. You led me to believe Brad didn't really want anything. And now I come to find out, he wanted it all."

Tears filled her eyes and she turned away, walking back into the kitchen. That was her default position. The kitchen was the center of her world. She went to the counter and turned to face him, hugging her arms in around herself.

"Jill," he said as he caught up with her. "I know this looks bad to you, but I didn't lie. When you asked, I just didn't answer."

"That's the same as a lie." She shook her head. "I can't trust you."

"Okay, Jill. I understand that you're really angry, and I'm sorry. But..."

She narrowed her eyes and hardened her

heart. "I think it's time for you to leave, Connor. Way past time."

He shook his head. Pain filled him, pain and regret. "Don't do this, Jill. Wait until you've calmed down. Think it over. I...I don't want to leave you here on your own."

"You have to. I can't trust you. I want you to go."

His eyes were tortured but she didn't relent. She had to have some time and space to think, to go over all that had happened in the last few days and decide if she could ever, ever talk to him again.

He winced. "You know that at some time soon, Brad will be coming, don't you?"

She blinked at him. "Why?"

"Because he wants those shares. He's not going to rest until he gets them. If he has to come here to do that, he will."

She was seething. "If you knew that, why didn't you tell me before? Why didn't you warn me?"

He had no answer for that.

"Go," she said. "You've helped me with some

things, but you've undermined me at the same time. I need you to go."

He started to say something, but she pointed toward the door. Shaking his head, he turned away. Then he looked back and said over his shoulder, "Call me if you need me," and he left.

She watched him walk away until tears flooded her eyes and she couldn't see anything anymore.

"Connor, Connor, how could you betray me like this?" she murmured.

The one person she thought she had in her corner, that she could count on when things got rough, the only one that she could really trust in this world besides Sara had turned out to be lying to her. And now it turned out all she had left was Sara.

She sank to the floor of the kitchen and hung her head and cried.

Connor was headed back to the mainland, but before he went, he had one last thing he had to do. He knew Sara lived only about a mile away, but her bungalow was right on the beach. Turning down the narrow road, he found her house easily. He'd been there before.

Walking up to the front door, he saw Sara in the side yard, trimming roses. He approached carefully but she still jumped when she saw him.

"Hey, Sara," he said. "We need to talk."

She backed away looking wary. "Connor, I don't want to talk to you. I already know how I feel about everything and I don't need you messing with my mind."

"Sara, come on. You know we both love Jill. Right?"

Sara made a face, but she nodded reluctantly.

"And you know that she's not going to let that baby go anywhere else, don't you? Not if she can help it."

Sara looked away.

"If you won't take her, your sister will. There's just no two ways about it."

Sara turned and looked at him pleadingly. "Can't you talk her out of it?"

"You know the answer to that. Nobody can talk her out of it." He looked down and kicked the dirt. "And we both know that taking on another baby is going to be hard. She doesn't need to have something that hard. She's already got far too much on her plate, far too much that she has to handle alone." He looked up at her. "So there's only one thing left to do. And you know what it is."

She shook her head with a jerky motion. Her face was a study in tragedy. "No," she said. "I can't."

He was quiet for a minute and she snipped off a few more dead blossoms. He listened to the water lapping against the shore not too far from where they stood. Seagulls called and a flock of low-flying pelicans swooped by.

Her hair was still slicked back into a bun at the back of her head. She'd changed into slacks and a fuzzy pullover, but she managed to look

like a fully functioning professional anyway.
There was something about her that spoke of
competence and dignity. But when he looked at
her face, all he saw was fear and sadness.

Finally he spoke to her quietly.

"Sara, come sit down with me."

She edged closer, but she still acted as though
she was afraid he might have something catching.

"Come on." He sat down on a wicker chair
and nodded toward the little wicker couch.
She walked over slowly and sat down, but she
wouldn't look at him.

"Thanks, Sara. I want to tell you about someone I got to know well in Singapore. Her name
is Sharon Wong. She's a very fine chef. A few
years ago, her neighbor died, leaving behind a
three-year-old girl. Sharon had gotten to know
them both during the neighbor's illness. She
took her broths and things and watched the
child for her at times.

"When the woman died, Social Services came

to take away the child, and Sharon realized what a nightmare that baby faced. Who knew who would end up caring for her? Maybe someone good. Maybe not. Maybe she would be in an institution for the rest of her childhood. She watched how the Social Services people treated that little girl and she made up her mind that she couldn't let this happen.

"So she stepped in and took the baby herself. When I met her, the girl was six years old, bright as a penny and sweet as candy. A delight. And Sharon told me that this little girl had enriched her life like nothing she'd ever dreamed might happen to her."

"And then she told me about a saying she'd heard lately. No one on their deathbed ever says they should have spent more time at the office. When you get down to what really counts, it's family."

Sara turned tragic eyes his way. "But I don't really have that kind of family," she said softly.

"Not now. But that doesn't mean you won't."

She stared at him, shaking her head. "Connor, if I had a choice right now between having a terrific career, or meeting a terrific guy, I'd take the career. I've had enough disappointment with terrific guys."

He shrugged as he rose to leave. "Guys are one thing. Babies are another." Reaching over, he kissed her cheek. She didn't turn away. She caught his hand and held it for a moment, looking deep into his eyes.

"See you later, Sara. Do the right thing, okay?"

And he walked away.

Jill was wandering through her house like a ghost. It was after dark and she hadn't put on any of the downstairs lights yet. The boys were in bed and sound asleep. She was alone.

Her mind was a jumble of thoughts, none of them very coherent. She was so angry with Connor, and at the same time, she was so hurt that he would still be on Brad's side after all he'd seen her go through. Why had he come all the way back just to prove to her that she really wanted him—only to say, "Sorry, I'm with Brad. He's such an old friend." That thought made her furious all over again.

She heard the front door opening and she stopped in her tracks, heart beating wildly. Who was this going to be?

"Anybody home?"

She let her held breath out in a whoosh. It was Sara.

Seconds later, Sara came into the family room where Jill was standing.

"What's going on? How come no lights?"

She wasn't going to tell her it was to hide her swollen eyes and tear-stained face. She would see that for herself soon enough.

Sara went ahead and turned on the overhead without asking permission. It must have seemed a natural thing to do.

"Hey, Jill. I've got to talk to you." Compared

to the last time Jill had seen her, she seemed to be brimming with energy.

Slowly Jill shook her head, staying to the shadows as much as she could. "Sara, sweetie, not now."

She thought Sara would notice from her voice that this was not a good time, but no. Sara charged ahead as though she hadn't said a thing.

"Wait. I'm sure you're busy, but this will just take a minute and it may help take a load off your mind."

Jill threw up her hands in surrender. "Anything that will do that," she muttered and tried to smile. "What is it?"

Sara came and stood before her, looking as earnest as Jill had ever seen her look.

"I've thought about this long and hard. I've looked at all the angles. And I've decided. I want to take Kelly's baby."

That was a jolt from the blue. "What are you saying? You can't possibly do that and take the job in L.A. Can you?"

"No." She shook her head. "I'm turning the job down."

"What? Oh, Sara, no!"

"Yes. A job is just a job. A baby is a human being. And this human being is even a part of our family, whether we like it or not." She smiled. "And I've decided to like it."

It was true that she looked much better, much healthier, than she had earlier that day when she had been so frightened of the entire concept. That was good. If it was really going to last.

She took her sister's hands in hers. "But, Sara, why?"

"It's a funny thing. I wanted a traditional life so badly. I planned my wedding from the time I was five years old. You know that. But every romance I tried to have ended badly. I just couldn't seem to find a man who fit me. I finally got hurt one too many times and I gave up all that. It's just too painful. No more romance. No more man who was wrong for me."

Jill nodded. She'd been there and watched it

all. "I know all this. But what does it have to do with taking the baby?"

"I decided maybe I was going at it from the wrong side. Maybe if I find a baby who fits me, I'll have my family without having to find a man first."

Oh, no. Sara had lost her mind.

"Sara, babies don't provide miracles. Please don't go into this thinking it's going to be a piece of cake. Don't depend on a baby to make you happy, to solve all your problems."

She waved that away. "Oh, please, Jill. Give me some credit. I know that. I've been with you enough with the twins to know that raising a child is no picnic."

"You got that right."

"But anyway, you're the one who always picks up the slack for everyone else. You do your big sister routine and go all noble on me, and I let you, because then I get out of doing things I don't want to do."

"Oh, Sara, please. We're not kids anymore."

"No, but we're still sisters." She gave Jill a hug. "So I decided. It's time I took my turn. I want Kelly's baby."

Jill took a deep breath and realized, suddenly what a weight she'd been carrying. "Oh, Sara, I hope you know what you're doing."

"I do."

She hugged her again and held her close, then leaned back and looked at her. "What changed your mind? What made you see it that way?"

"Connor."

"Connor?" She was thunderstruck.

She heaved a heavy sigh. "Yes, it was Connor. He gave me a good talking-to and then told me about a friend of his. Some woman in Singapore…"

"Sharon Wong?"

"That's the one. Do you know her?"

"No."

"Well, he sat me down and made me take a more realistic look at life."

"He did?" Jill felt dizzy.

"Yeah. Where is he?"

"He's a…"

"You know, that is one great guy. You'd better not let him slip away. He's a treasure." She looked around the room and toward the back porch. "So where is he, anyway?"

"I, uh, he left."

Her head swung around. "Left? Where did he go? What happened?"

"I told him to leave."

"Oh, Jill… You didn't!"

"I did. I told him to go. I was so angry."

"Why?"

She took a deep breath and tried to remember it all, including the incredible pain she'd felt. Quickly she explained to Sara about the loan being called, and how Connor thought Brad was behind it. Then she went on to fill in her problems with Connor.

"He didn't tell me the truth about what Brad wanted and when I found out that he wanted me to sell him the shares I swore I would never give up, I just…I felt like he was manipulating me. Like I couldn't trust him. Like he was on Brad's side again. Why didn't he prepare me to know what Brad was up to?"

"You think he's on Brad's side?"

Jill nodded.

Sara stared at her. "What are you, nuts? You do realize he's crazy in love with you, don't you?"

She shook her head. "Sara, I don't think—"

"You can see it in the way he looks at you."

She hesitated. "Do you really think so?"

"Come on, he's always had a crush on you. And now I think it's developed into full-blown mad love. He's insanely in love with you."

Jill was feeling dizzy again. "We've always been friends."

"No. It's more than that." Sara threw up her hands. "He wants you, babe. Don't let that one get away."

"I just got so frustrated. And…and so jealous."

"Jealous?"

She nodded. "I mean—is he my friend or Brad's? It makes a difference."

Sara nodded wisely. "I told him that the first day he was here. I told him if he was going to be your friend, he had to get rid of Brad. And you know what? He was ready to do it."

Jill wasn't so sure. Sara could go off like a runaway train at times. But she listened to her sister and they talked about how she was going to manage to take care of a baby, and after she left, she went back over what she'd said about Connor and she felt more confused than ever.

There was no doubt about it, she wanted Connor back. For the past couple of days, he'd been her shelter against the storm. Why on earth was she making him go?

But maybe it was for the best. After all, she didn't want him to be here if he was Brad's friend more than he was hers. What was the truth? She was overwhelmed by the emotions churning inside her.

But she knew one thing: it was time to face

facts. She loved Connor. She'd probably loved him for years and hadn't been able to admit it to herself. But she could remember countless times that she'd been frustrated with Brad and wished he could be more like Connor. She'd known forever that Connor fit her better than Brad did. They looked at life through much the same lens. They liked the same things, laughed at the same jokes. Brad always seemed restless and disapproving. Why had she put up with it for so long?

And Connor was so darn sexy. She'd always felt a certain buzz around him. Brad was more demanding, more dominant. Connor was more easygoing. More her type. What a fool she'd been all these years.

She loved Connor. Wow.

Except for one little tiny problem. No matter what Sara said, she was pretty sure he didn't love her. He liked her fine, he always had. But he liked a lot of girls. And when push came to shove, he was better friends with Brad than he was with her. And that hurt.

In fact, it cut deep. Brad had been so awful to her. It had taken time, but she'd finally come to a place where she could look into the past and face the truth. She'd been blinded by a lot of things when she'd thought she loved Brad. A lot of those things were not too flattering to her. She'd been a fool. Now she could look Brad squarely in the eye and say, "Brad, you're a real jerk." At least, she thought she could.

She had to get that out of her system because, like it or not, Brad was her boys' father. There was no hiding from that. Even Brad couldn't pretend it didn't matter. They would always be tied to him in ways he couldn't control.

So Connor had tried to help her in his way, and now she'd kicked him out. Maybe that wasn't the wisest thing to do, but she couldn't pretend with Connor. She was in love with him. What if he knew that? What if he saw it in her face, in her reactions? Would he use it against her?

She didn't know, because she really couldn't trust him.

Why hadn't he told her the truth right from the beginning so that she could get prepared for any sort of attack from Brad? Now she was going to have to deal with Brad on her own.

That was going to be hard to do. Brad had a domineering way about him and she'd been trained over the years to yield to him. It almost came naturally to her. She was going to have to fight against that impulse. She couldn't let him walk all over her. And once he realized she wasn't going to obey him, what next? He would find some way to make her pay. Brad was capable of doing almost anything.

Life was becoming impossible. What was she going to do? She was probably going to lose her house and lose her business. She couldn't meet the loan call. She was going to go under like a small boat in heavy swells.

The only way out she could see was to sell her shares to Brad. She didn't want to do it.

She especially hated to do anything that might make him happy. But she wasn't going to have any choice. Her options had just become even more limited.

Well, she might end up that way, but she intended to put up a fight as long as she could. She would see how well she could stand up to Brad when she really tried. Live and learn.

In the meantime, all she could do was sit here and wait for Brad to show up.

CHAPTER TEN

CONNOR CHECKED BACK into his hotel. As he
started for the elevators, he heard "Mambo!"
coming from the dining room dance floor and
he couldn't resist looking in to see if Karl was
back. Sure enough, and dancing with a bewildered looking redhead. Connor ducked back
out quickly. He didn't want to scare Karl off.

He ordered something from room service and
watched the news and then he turned off the TV
and went out and walked the Seattle streets for
a couple of hours. This was a city he knew well.
He'd grown up not far away in a small town,
and then gone to the University. The years after
college had been spent right here. It was home
in a sense. He could live here. He didn't need
anything else.

Except Jill. He needed Jill more than he needed air to breathe.

His cell received a text and he flipped it out to see who it was. Brad had finally answered him.

"You're right," he said. "I need to come and get what I need myself. I'll be there in the morning."

So Brad was coming to work his magic on Jill. What did he think—that he could walk in and hypnotize her into doing things his way? Or was he ready to give her what she'd always wanted—marriage and a promise to try to be a father to his kids?

That night he couldn't sleep. He spent the time staring at the ceiling and going over what had happened over the last few days. He knew he was following a familiar pattern. He'd begun to let his feelings for Jill come out and actually show themselves, but once Jill backed away, so did he. He'd walked off and left the field to Brad so many times, it seemed the natural thing to do.

But it wasn't. It was time he made up his mind, declared himself, and claimed Jill for himself. This was probably his last chance to do it. What the hell was he waiting for?

Damn it, she needed him. He was the only one who loved her the way she needed to be loved. He was the only one ready to protect her and make her happy, the only one who was ready to help her raise her kids. The only other person he needed to convince was Jill herself. And that was the only part he was still a little shaky on.

He was a realist and he knew there was a chance that Brad would offer to take Jill back, and he knew there was a chance she would take him up on it. She yearned to have the boys' father back fulfilling his role, giving them what they needed. Whether she yearned for the man himself in the same way, he wasn't sure. But he wasn't going to let things take their natural course and see what happened. No. Not this time. He was going to fight for the woman he loved.

He ate an early breakfast in the coffee shop and then he headed for the ferry landing. He got out of the car during the crossing and looked up at the house Jill and Brad had bought together when their marriage was young and the company was all they cared about. How quickly things could change.

He was pretty sure Brad would show up sometime today. And how Jill reacted to that would tell the tale. He meant to play a part, regardless. And if he had to tell a few home truths to his old friend, he was ready to do it. He drew in a lungful of sea air and began to prepare for what he was going to do.

Jill had the children up and dressed and ready to go first thing in the morning. She'd hardly slept at all but she had done a lot of thinking. She was definitely staring at a fork in her life's road. Would she bow to Brad, or would she fight for Connor? Could she find a way to make Connor want her more than he wanted to be friends with Brad? If she couldn't do that, it was all over. But if she didn't even try, how would she ever know?

She planned to leave the twins with Sara and then she was heading to the mainland. She was going to go and find Connor and tell him she loved him. Her blood pounded in her ears. She was so scared. But she had to take the chance. Like Sara said, she couldn't let him slip away.

She'd let the boys out to play in the backyard while she got things ready and she was just about to get them and put them into the car when she heard the front door close. She stopped, listening.

"Sara?" she called at last. "Is that you?"

There was no answer. She swallowed hard, glancing toward the side door and thinking of making a run for it, one child under each arm. But before she could try that out, Brad appeared in the doorway to the kitchen.

"No," he said, watching her coolly. "It's me."

* * *

It was still early and once Connor got across the channel, he decided to take a run around the island before he went up to the house. The trip was as pretty as it had ever been, with trees and a lush growth of flowers that was almost tropical in its glory. What a wonderful place to choose to raise a family.

As he came back around, he stopped at a light and looked down at the ferry landing. The next one had arrived, and the first car coming off was a silver Porsche. He knew right away that had to be Brad.

Staying where he was, he watched as the car climbed the hill and turned into Jill's driveway, then parked in front of the entryway. Brad got out and headed for the front door, and Connor gritted his teeth and counted to ten. He had to force back the rage that threatened to overwhelm him. If he came face-to-face with Brad right now, he would surely end up bloodying the man's nose. He had to give it a minute.

Once he was calmer, he turned his car up toward the house, parking on the street. He got out just as he saw Brad disappearing inside.

Striding quickly up the hill, he went around back, quietly opening the door to the screened-in porch, which opened onto the kitchen. Ten to one she would be there. He stopped and listened.

Jill was shaking. She only hoped Brad couldn't tell. How many times had she imagined this scene? Here he was, in the flesh.

This was the first time he'd been back to their house since the divorce. The first time she'd seen him in over a year. She shoved her unruly hair back behind her ears and tried to smile.

"It's good to see you, Brad," she said breathlessly.

His eyes had been cold as steel when he'd first come in, but as she watched, they began to warm. "Jill," he said, and held out his hands to her.

She hesitated for a few seconds, but she took them. They were warm. He was so cool and confident. And here she was, rattled and skittish as a baby bird.

"I've missed you," he said.

She blinked at him. Why did his lies always sound so sincere?

"Where's Connor?" he asked.

"Oh, he...he left. Last night."

"Ah," he said, and she could tell he thought Connor had left because he was coming. "Probably a good thing," he said almost to himself. "Did he ever give you my message?" he asked.

She took a deep breath. "Why don't you just tell me what that message is?"

"I don't want to rush things. How about a cup of coffee while we talk over old times?"

He was so cool, so ready to treat her like dirt and pretend she deserved it. She dug deep inside. She couldn't let him maneuver her. This was her home and he was the invader.

"I...I don't have any coffee ready," she told

him. "Why don't you just get on with it? I'd like to know where we stand."

He didn't like that. She could see the annoyance flash in his eyes. "Okay," he said shortly. "Here's the deal. I need those shares, Jill. You have fifteen percent of my company. I'm going to have to ask for them back."

"Really? And what if I want to keep them?"

He looked as though he could hardly believe she was being so obstinate. "No, don't you understand? I need them. I'm fighting off a mini rebellion and I need them to regain the advantage." He frowned. He could see she wasn't bending for him the way he thought she should. "Listen, I'll make it worth your while. I'm prepared to pay you quite handsomely for them."

He named a figure that didn't sound all that handsome to her. If he could pay that for shares, why couldn't he pay child support? But she knew the answer to that. Because he didn't want to.

"I'm being attacked by some of the other

shareholders who are conspiring against me. I need those shares to defend myself. And of course, if you ever hope to get any more money out of me, you'd better help."

She found herself staring at him. The fear had melted away. He was just a big jerk. There was no reason to let him intimidate her.

"Brad, I'm not interested in selling. I feel that those shares are a legacy of sorts for the boys. I want them to be there for them when they grow up, both as an investment and for traditional reasons."

His jaw tightened. "All right, I'll double the offer."

She shook her head. "But that's not the point. I want the boys to have something from their father. I'm just sorry you don't feel the same way."

"Are you crazy? What do those brats have to do with my company?"

She glared at him. Didn't he have any human feelings at all? "We built that company together, you, me and Connor. It was a work of joy and friendship between us all at the time."

"That's a crock. I had the idea, I worked out the plans, I did the development. You two were filler. The company is mine. You had very little to do with it." He grunted. "And those kids didn't have anything to do with it."

Her fingers were trembling but she was holding firm. "Whether or not you want to acknowledge them, those kids are yours. They have your DNA. They wouldn't exist without you. Though you may never be a real father to them, this will give them something to know about you, to feel they've been given a gift from you."

"That's ridiculous. It's sentimental garbage." He shook his head as though he just couldn't understand her attitude. "Jill, what's happened to you? You were once my biggest supporter. You would have done anything to help me. And now…"

For just a moment she remembered him as he used to be, so young and handsome, with the moonlight in his eyes and a kiss on his mind. She thought of how it was when they were first married and he had let her know how much he wanted her, every minute of the day. She'd thought it would always be like that. She'd been wrong.

But thinking about what used to be had the effect of cooling her anger. They did have a past. She couldn't ignore that. She took a deep breath and made her voice softer, kinder, more understanding.

"Brad, I did support you for so many years. But what you've done has undermined that. Lately you have done nothing but stand in my way. And you expect me to bend over backward for you?"

He controlled his own anger and tried to smile. "You know what, you're right. And that wasn't really fair of me." He tried to look sincere. "But everything I do is for the good of the company. You know that."

She shrugged. That wasn't good enough to justify what he'd done.

He stared at her for a long moment, then nodded and adjusted his stance. He was good at sizing up the other side and finding a way to adapt to new facts.

"Okay, Jill. I understand. You need something more." He nodded, thinking for a moment. "Here's the deal. I want full ownership of the company. I need it. I'm willing to take you back to get it."

She almost fell over at his words. "You'll take me back?"

"Yes, I will."

Unbelievable. "And the boys?"

He turned and looked at the twins playing on the hill behind the house. "Is that them?"

She nodded.

"Sure, why not?" He turned back, his eyes hard and cold as steel. "Have we got a deal?"

She stared at him. What could she say? Did she have a right to hand away her children's connection with their father? But what was that connection worth? Why hadn't she ever seen the depths of his vile selfishness before? His soul was corrupt.

"Brad, you've really surprised me with this. I never thought you would make such an offer."

"So what do you say?"

"She says 'no.'" Suddenly Connor was in the room with them.

"Hello, Brad," he said, his tone hard and icy. "She says 'no deal.' Sorry."

She looked from Brad to Connor and back again, confused. Where had he come from? She wasn't sure, but suddenly he was there and suddenly Brad didn't look so smooth and sure of himself.

"Connor," Brad said, looking annoyed. "I thought you were gone."

"I was. But I'm back."

Brad looked unsure. "This is just a matter between me and Jill."

"No, it's not. I'm afraid there's been a change."

Connor stood balanced, his stance wide, like a fighter. In every way, he was exuding a toughness she didn't think she'd ever seen in him before. "I'm involved now."

Brad looked bewildered. "What the hell are you talking about?"

"You're not married to Jill anymore. In fact, since you won't acknowledge your own children, and from what I understand, you hardly ever give them any money, the only real substantial tie they have with you is those shares."

He turned and looked at Jill. "Here's my advice. Give him the shares. Let him buy them from you. Once they're gone, and you and I are married, he won't have any reason left to contact you in any way or have any part in your life. You'll be free of him." He reached out and touched her shoulder. "But of course, it's up to you. What do you say?"

Jill stared at Connor. She heard his words but she was having some trouble understanding them. Did he mean…? Wait, what did he say about marrying her? A bubble began to rise in her chest—a bubble of happiness. She wanted to dance and laugh and sing, all at once.

"Connor?" she said, smiling at him in wonder. "Are you feeling okay?"

He gave her a half smile back. "I'm feeling fine. How about you?"

"I think I'm going to faint." She reached out and he caught hold, steadying her against him. She put an arm around his waist and pulled even closer, looking up at him with laughter bubbling out all over.

He gazed down at her and grinned. He had a good feeling about how this was turning out. There was only one last test. Was she ready to cut all ties to Brad? "What do you think about selling back the shares?" he asked her.

She nodded happily. Suddenly she knew that she just didn't care about the shares. All her excuses had been hogwash meant to give her an excuse to not do what Brad wanted. But she didn't care about that anymore. She didn't have to care about Brad. She was going to care about her family, and he wasn't in it. He'd given up that chance long ago.

"I think you're right," she said. "I liked that second offer."

Brad looked uncertain.

Connor shrugged at him. "There you go. Hand over the money, Brad. Let's see the glint of your gold."

"Hey, she just said…"

"I don't care what you heard. She'll take the second offer. Or would you rather have her contact the people in the company who are fighting you and see how much they'll offer?"

Brad frowned at him, shooting daggers of hate, but he pulled out his checkbook. He wrote out a check and handed it to Jill. She looked at it, held it up to the light, then nodded and put it down, leaving the room to get her documentation. In a moment she was back.

"Here are the shares," she said. "There you

go. It's all you now, Brad. You don't need me for anything anymore. Right?"

Brad didn't say a word.

"Let's make a pact," Jill said. "Let's not see each other ever again. Okay?"

He seemed completely bewildered. "Jill. Don't you remember what we once had together?"

She snorted. "Don't you remember what you did to me eighteen months ago?"

One last disgruntled look and Brad headed for the door. Connor pulled Jill into his arms and smiled down at her.

"I hope you don't feel like I coerced you into that."

"Not at all. I think it was the perfect solution. If he'd come and asked me in a humble, friendly way, I would have handed them back to him at any time. It was just when he acted like such a jerk, I couldn't stand the thought of giving in to him."

"At least you made him pay for them."

She shook her head and laughed. "It is so worth it to get him out of my life."

He searched her dark eyes. "You're sure there's nothing left? You don't love him?"

"How can you even ask that?" She touched his face with her fingertips. "I love you," she said, her voice breaking on the word. "It's taken a while to get that through my skull, but it's true."

He shook his head, laughing softly. "That's quite a relief. I wasn't sure."

She smiled and snuggled into his arms. "I'm not even going to ask if you still consider Brad your best friend. Actions speak louder than words. You showed me."

"You're my best friend," he told her lovingly.

She pursed her lips, looking up at him with her brows drawn together. "And the new baby?" she asked, just testing reality. "Are you really willing to take that one on with me?"

"Of course. It's going to be crazy around here with all these kids, but I think I can handle it."

He went to the sliding glass door and called the boys and they came running.

"Well," Jill said, "the truth is, Kelly's baby is going to be living with Sara."

He turned and looked at her. "Ah. She came around, did she?"

"Thanks to you."

He shook his head. "She was going to get there eventually. It just took some time for the shock to wear off."

Jill looked at him with stars in her eyes. He was so good and so ready to be a part of this family and commit to them all, even to her sister. And the new baby. She hardly knew how to contain her happiness.

The twins roared in and headed for the sunroom and she went back into Connor's arms. This was where she really belonged. This is where she was going to stay. Forever was a long, long time, but she was ready to promise it.

"I love you," she whispered to him.

"I've always loved you," he told her, his gaze dark with adoration and longing. "So I win."

"Oh, no, my handsome husband-to-be. If anyone is a winner here, it's me." And she kissed him hard, just to make sure he knew it.

* * * * *